JUNGLE GODDESS

I0525924

by

CHARLES NUETZEL

WRITING AS "DAVID JOHNSON"

The Borgo Press
An Imprint of Wildside Press

MMVII

Dedicated to my
personal goddess,

Brigitte

SECOND EDITION

CONTENTS

INTRODUCTION

This book goes back to basics, I suppose, in so many ways. Really back to before I was even thinking about writing. This was the time of the Hardy Boy books and compulsive reading. This is when I discovered the Mars books by Edgar Rice Burroughs. When I picked up *A Princess of Mars* and read the opening lines, I was instantly hooked. That led, over the following months and years, to discovering all the worlds of ERB.

Then, many years later, I became a writer and remembered the thrilling adventures that had become a major part of my reading experience for so long.

Tarzan, of course, had already captured me on film, but that wasn't very serious stuff; it was in the books that I discovered the real thing. Back then the moral codes were very strict and women always sought to kill themselves rather than face *a fate worse than death*. For a respectable woman, love and sex were something to save for marriage!

I began to wonder, as a published writer, what a female growing up in the jungle like Tarzan had would be really like. Certainly sex would be simply a normal part of life—not something to avoid at all cost!

That sounded intriguing. What if a guy discovered this young jungle girl, and what if he was an adventure writer of great fame, and what if he was in reality somewhat of your normal, run-in-the-mill kinda cowardly guy, totally different from the character the public thought him to be? What if he had been crash-landed in the middle of the African jungle and what if....

Oh, so many what ifs.

I immediately sat down and started writing. And then stopped halfway through the book. For some reason it lay unfinished in my files for, perhaps, a year. Then when I needed a book to fill a publishing demand, I yanked it out and finished it off!

It came out as *Jungle Nymph* by David Johnson, and then later, having done its duty in translation in Europe, became the second half of a double book, *Jungle Jungle* (carrying my own byline), put out by Powell Publications under its present title: *Jungle Goddess*.

What is now presented under this same title is a slightly different version, updated and somewhat expanded. And I offer it within a new framework that seems, to me, far more interesting.

It is the same story of a young jungle girl, the cowardly famous adventure writer and a couple of nice ladies along with the required "white hunter" to show them the way!

And of course savage beasts and wild natives all out to get 'em!

Well that just about tells it all, except for the story itself.

—CHARLES NUETZEL
Thousand Oaks, California
July 2006

CHAPTER 1

Off to Africa

The events leading up to the recent release of BOB LAKE AND THE JUNGLE GODDESS started several years before its publication. For those who lived these earlier adventures they were even more fantastic than what was reported in the bestselling book. For Carol Hill it all began with....

"I want that assignment in Africa—with Bob Lake!" she announced, once in the publisher's large book-lined office. She looked at Henry Turner with hard determination in her eyes. She had insisted on this audience with her boss, determined to make a hard sell for this prime ticket to fame.

It was one of those places where few people made demands—but many had taken commands from the heavy, barrel-chested man sitting behind the large oak desk. He owned the company and everybody who worked there. For some two years, now, she'd been working her way up to the point where it was possible to reach out for this kind of assignment.

Strangely enough the man had been more than

willing to see her, though his chubby face revealed little as to what he was really thinking. Yet his eyes had swept over her as if wanting to make a feast of what he saw. Nothing more.

"I want it, and I'd be good at it!" she added when the silence met her opening statement. "With Bob Lake!"

It was almost a demand. Soon she would have second thoughts. But at that moment she was determined to get this quick chance for real recognition. And proof she could make it big in a man's world.

Henry Turner's gray eyes studied the blonde in front of him. There was a hard calculating coldness in his gaze as it once again swept over trim body. And something which almost offered: *and what are you willing to do for me to get this assignment?* His voice was just edging on amusement as he said: "So?"

"I want it, Henry!" Carol announced again, mentally wishing, for this one time in her life, she *wasn't* a woman. Henry Turner had tried to bed her since the first day she'd started work at the *Turner Publishing Company.* Carol was a photographer, *not* a tramp. It was the only line she'd never crossed in getting ahead. She wouldn't sleep her way to the top—but the so-called glass ceiling against females wouldn't hold her back. Very early in life she'd decided to put everything aside, motherhood, marriage, in favor of making a real name for herself as a photographer.

"I mean that! I really want it!" Carol stated in an aggressive manner.

"You serious?" Henry Turner demanded. "I don't believe you!" But there was little conviction in his voice. He was playing a blunt game, and she was

8

expected to play it out. He liked to manipulate.

"I'm deadly serious!" she told him. "I've always wanted to go to Africa. And shooting a Bob Lake book would be a pretty creative challenge!"

"That's *no* assignment for a woman." Turner retorted. There was only a hint of mockery in his voice.

"That's bull!" Carol pointed out, smiling, forcing herself to play into his game. Maybe he just wanted a hard sell. "And I'd do a bang-up job. Just like in Miami!"

Henry wiped imaginary sweat from his forehead. Slowly standing, he stepped around the desk.

"Rita Bentley is backing the trip. You know her reputation."

"Sure. Doesn't everybody? Tab Queen of the Day & Night!"

"Some of that tabloid stuff is true."

"And the rest is garbage!" she counter. "And I know the rumors, too. Devours her men!"

They both laughed a bit stiffly.

"And very possessive! She savagely attack a woman who flirted with one of her boy-toys."

"I don't flirt!" Carol announced. "Nor play around."

"Well, true enough. Sad to say." His eyes studied hers, and then swept along her body as if mentally caressing it.

"Don't even think it, *Mister* Turner!" she laughed good-naturedly. "Don't mix pleasure with business."

The man chuckled at that. "For all I know you don't mix pleasure with anything."

"I wouldn't bet on that!" She winked playfully.

9

"Quite frankly, I have more important things to focus on!"

"Using the lens, I assume!" he mused. "Yes, one of the best masters of that fine art!"

"Well, we agree on something, don't we?" she stated in mocked seriousness.

He considered her for a moment then shrugged: "Perhaps you'd get along with Ms Bentley."

"Try me!" Carol challenged.

The man shrugged, as if having resigned himself.

"Okay, okay! If you insist!" His hands leaned on the desk, fingers just touching a large envelope lying there. "It's your headache. Bob can be a pain. I guess you know how *he* works!"

"With a bottle in one hand and a woman in the other!" Carol said evenly. "And Rita is a possessive lady. And Loony, to boot! I know all the nasty rumors. Nut house junky."

"Those weren't just rumors. The breakdown was real. Even if many years ago."

"Everybody visits Shrinkland nowadays!"

They both laughed at that, then the man grew serious, nodded: "Okay. Play her right and you shouldn't have any trouble! Like walking on eggs."

"I'm a good egg walker, boss!" she laughed a bit too lightly. "And what Rita wants, Rita gets! I have no designs on anybody or thing...but a notch in my career!"

He nodded, all business. "You are to meet Ms Bentley in Nairobi in three days. She's hired *Barton & Gordon Ltd* to run the safari. I've known them for years. John Barton plays Big White Hunter and Allen

Gordon runs the office. Barton will find a nice jungle setting and set up a camp. I want motion pictures and stills. All the kills—get them on film. Make it look like Bob did it all himself—regardless."

Carol merely nodded, said nothing.

Turner sighed and then tapped the large envelope lying on his desk. "This is all you need as background and…as you see, has your name on it…"

She merely smiled, saying nothing. So he had set her up to beg!

Carol was only slightly annoyed at having been manipulated.

"I've already sent Charlie on another job—he doesn't give a damn where he gets his pay check."

"I guess you had your fun," she admitted, taking the envelop with her name on it. "Made me *convince* you!"

"Why not? I wanted to be sure about you. So…report to Lake—the two of you leave by plane tomorrow night!"

* * * * * * *

The long fight to Nairobi was a study in anguished boredom to Bob Lake. He was deep in a psychological depression that gnawed at his guts. It was more than a mere hangover. He was on an old mental treadmill! All these years he had written fictionalized adventures that he wasn't really capable of living. The closest thing he'd come to actual physical action was boxing in the local gym as a teenager and later as a young man. It was a hobby, safely tucked away in a strange part of his brain—real but mere game playing;

not serious combat. Everybody thought he actually was the action hero of his books. Boxing was the only action he'd ever taken, though within the confines of a totally control ring and gym. But now he was trapped into actually living out a real life adventure! *Bob Lake on Safari.* That party at the Rita Bentley's had doomed him. With Henry Turner standing there with them, she had sprung her trap when talking about her coming trip to Africa.

Bob had never wanted to hit a woman before that moment.

"Why don't you go with us?" Rita almost pleaded, gripping his arm excitedly, her eyes flashing with intimate promise.

"You kidding, of course!" Bob gulped. The last place he had ever wanted to go was Africa. And she knew it!

"Oh, honey, I don't kid about anything!" she murmured, giving him a peck on the cheek, while long fingernails dug painfully into his forearm. "I want you with me! And you can do a book about our adventures. Not *all* of them, of course."

"We've been through all that," he pointed out. "You know how I feel!"

She had suggested it once before in private and Bob thought he'd convinced her of his lack of interest. But, if Rita wanted something bad enough she got it!

"Oh, Bob, don't be silly. Just think: all expenses paid by yours truly! *On Safari with Rita Bentley Queen of the Tabloids*!"

That's when Henry Turner exclaimed: "She's right! Why not? It'd be a swell idea for your next book! Though not that title, thank you!"

"Oh, then call it: *Bob Lake & Rita Bentley's Erotic Africa*!" Rita suggested. "Whatever you want. I don't care!"

"*Bob Lake on Safari* works for me!" the publisher announced, as if that closed the issue.

The woman considered Turner for a moment, and then shrugged. "Just so I get mentioned inside! Maybe Bob can reveal the real Rita Bentley—well, not everything, of course. Just the nice stuff! And there's plenty of nice stuff...in me!"

She laughed at that as if it were a joke. "And, Mr. Turner, dear Hank, it'll cost just a minor mention in the book itself about our adventures together in Dark Africa, which isn't quite as dark as it used to be."

"Not what I heard," Turner noted. "There still are places our modern civilization haven't touched."

"Oh, poo, as they say. Modern safaris are a camp in the park. When the hunt's on it is the Big White Bwana Hunter who does all the work, letting the clients take all the credit. Nothing to worry about. Think about it, my offer. I'm very serious."

Turner, who was always quick to pick up a margin of profit, leaped at the bait: "That's a deal breaker, Ms Bentley."

When Bob was once again alone with Rita, he said: "Damn you, he thinks you're serious!"

"I am! Why do you think I arranged this party, inviting your publisher?" she asked, continuing on without giving him a chance to answer. "You work too hard on those books. Gotta get out more often with the real natives!"

That sounded ominous. He'd been careful when "off on an adventure" to hide away where nobody

13

could find him. She couldn't know the truth.

Rita smiling mysteriously, said: "Oh, come on Bob, it'll be great fun! You'll see!"

He was trapped.

She pouted cutely. "And like they say in the tabloids: *what Rita wants, Rita gets!* You know that!"

He knew all too well; as their relationship had proven. The woman was a wild in bed and he had claw marks on his back to prove it! A wildcat! But also temperamental as hell.

He had hoped the African thing would fade. He should have known better. The price of enjoying Rita's favor was submitting to her demands.

And several days later when Turner brought it up in his office there was no way out of it.

He'd been surprised about Carol Hill being assigned as photographer. They'd never worked together. She was a very ambitious, driven woman, totally different than Rita. Carol was blonde, Rita dark. Carol was all business. Rita all play. Carol hadn't slept her way up; pure talent had blazed her success. Yet most men considered her slim, curving good looks quite delightful. Hardly the type any man would turn down if she were to throw herself at him. Fat chance of that happening with Carol. He wondered what it would take to bed that lady.

Bob mused over that image then shrugged it off: *Carol Hill was off limits, in any case.*

Right now Rita was his assignment. Henry Turner had made that very clear.

Turner had said: "Play her. I know her rep for being easily bored and fickle. Make sure she's a happy camper!"

14

"I know how to handle Rita," he assured the man. His hands squeezed the air in front of him in a very bluntly suggestive way. "A little of that and a bottle of wine keeps her warm and ripe for the picking."

"Don't be silly. She's a sophisticated lady. She can be a rough ride if crossed. So while she has her hooks in ya, you best not wiggle the wrong way cause it might be painful!"

"Don't worry. The kind of wiggling I'll do makes her delirious!" Which was true. Even if her long nails enjoyed biting deep into his flesh at moments of intense passion. Both of them liked a casual relationship mixed with plenty of booze.

Turner chuckled. "Well, good for you. Have fun. I envy you."

That had ended the conversation, but not his sense of fear.

He knew that in time his secret would be out. He couldn't keep it forever locked up in that mountain cabin where he did most of his writing.

Maybe this was a chance to expand his horizons!

He tried to convince himself.

Chances were that Rita was right about it being a piece of cake. So if he could fake out the next days under the safe cover of this commercial safari, things might not be too bad. Technically he knew all the terms and all the facts necessary to write about such travels; on paper he'd been convincing. Now he simply had to translate knowledge into action. For years he had been faking it; for years he had perfected the outward image of the man of action. Now he was being presented with the greatest acting challenge in his life.

Maybe things would work out okay he kept saying over and over, like a mantra.

CHAPTER 2

Storm Warnings

Finally they arrived at the Nairobi airport and were met by a native servant who had been instructed to take them to the house that Rita had rented.

Neither Bob nor Carol talked during the ride through Nairobi. Finally the driver pulled the car up to a large white house. A few moments later Rita greeted them in the living room of the expensively furnished bungalow. After introductions, Rita turned to Carol and said: 'I hope you will enjoy yourself."

She paused, then added: "I'm surprised that Turner sent a woman on this trip." There was just the cutting edge of stiffness to her voice.

"Oh, I wanted it," Carol explained brightly. "I literally begged for the job!"

"Well, I guess you would like to freshen up a bit. One of the servants will take you to your room." She indicated a handsome young native with the nod of her head and gave him instructions. "And see that Miss Hill gets everything she wants...well not *every-thing*..." The woman's eyes moved possessively to Bob, then returned to Carol: "Just be sure she gets everything she…*needs!*"

When the other woman had left, Rita turned to Bob. "It's going to be a lot of fun! What a thrill!"

"Yes…" Bob managed, hiding the nervous twinge running down his spine.

"I've always wanted to see you in action." she teased, planting a kiss on his cheek.

"Don't expect too much!" he suggested, vaguely. "Reputations are never what they seem in the papers."

"I know all about that, for sure!" she nodded, shrugged, "Doesn't really matter to me. Just be nice having you around for a few weeks—just the two of us."

"And all the safari personnel?"

"They *really* don't count!" Then as an after thought she said: "Just so that Ms Hill isn't hounding you with her cameras—or *anything* else."

"She business, nothing more," Bob promised; then teased her with: "Sad to say!"

"She better not be! You're *all* mine! And I'm a *jealous* property owner!" That last was followed by a rather harsh, edgy laugh. "I don't let *anybody* trespass on my territory!"

Rita reached out and touched his arm affectionately. "Want a drink?"

"That's a hell of a good idea!"

"Follow me," Rita instructed. Then added with a husky laugh: "We can drink and hungrily devour whatever catches our attention!"

The way her eyes swept over him left little to his imagination.

* * * * * * *

Bob was working on a hangover when he settled behind the copilot's seat of the small two-engine plane that was going to take them across the African jungle. The others were in the passenger's section, the door shut, giving the two men some sense of privacy.

He'd been invited to play co-pilot. He found that rather exciting. In fact, some elements of these last hours were almost exciting; appealing. He'd written about this kind of adventure, now he was being forced to actually live it. And, so far, it really wasn't that horrid. He hoped.

John Barton, sitting next to him, was large and broad, well muscled. His face had the mark of a man used to hard adventure, fast action and quick thinking. He appeared far more flashing in his "safari" clothes. Now the man was totally different from last night when dressed more formally. Bob realized that this was the kind of male animal Rita probably thought he was—the perfect man of action.

Here sat our Big Bwana, he thought, *our White Hunter and pilot; boss of the expedition.*

They had met the evening before. Carol and Barton had become friendly, but nothing more. The hunter seemed to almost ignore the women, merely being politely professional. In fact he'd said very little of a personal nature. But there was something about the way his eyes flinted from person to person, almost as if reading their thoughts that impressed Bob. For the most part the conversation had been fairly general; just the four of them sizing one another up for the coming adventure. He'd consumed, perhaps, a bit more booze than he should have, and much of his attention was forced to focus on Rita, who kept secretly touching him under the table from time to time. They'd all turned in early for this early morning start.

"Well, this is it, Bobby-boy!" Barton exclaimed, as he fired the engines and started the plane down the runway. In a few minutes they were reaching for the clouds.

The sky was clean as they took off from Nairobi, though in the next hours it suddenly began to change in texture.

"You sure everything is okay? I heard something about a storm." Bob cautioned in a dead sounding voice.

"Nothing to worry about. We should be able to climb above it, if it comes our way. As long as the plane keeps chuggin' there isn't a thing to worry about! I had some trouble with this ol' lady a year or so back, but we worked that out. And as you can see, I'm alive and well."

"Just so you keep us all in the same condition," Bob offered, a bit uncertain.

"Never you mind about that. If I had doubts I wouldn't be flying even if Ms Bentley was quite insistent about an immediate start! I got the impression one doesn't deny her anything she wants!" His broad face opened in a generous smile.

"You're right about that."

"Well, I never take a client I don't know something about. Your boss filled me in. Well, you'll have your hands full. Bet she's all tigresses! I'll take care of you folks. You can deal with Ms Bentley. She's yours to command."

"More like the other way around," Bob admitted, dryly.

"Well, that's fine with me." He laughed at that. Then added: "We're well equipped. And during the next days you'll be enjoying the thrills of a life-time!"

"I can do without too many thrills," Bob confessed, a bit nervously.

"You sound actually…uneasy. First time on safari?"

"First time."

"Well you're in for it. We have plenty of supplies and all the weapons we need to back us up—and quite frankly this is nothing but a soft-safari. Meaning, fun and games in jungle land!"

"Easy for you to say!"

"Believe me! Don't worry!"

"I'll try," Bob offered, without humor. "Just hope the storm warning is nothing more than…warnings!"

"Warning or not, don't worry, I've never lost a client…yet!"

"How long have you been at this?" he asked, conversationally, keeping down the sense of nervous fear. *Just play out the act, Bob*, he told himself. *After all, you aren't a damn coward; just inexperienced.*

"Most of my life. Born here, lived here and enjoyed here!" the man announced, pointing towards the ground. "Africa has been my life."

Impulsively, Bob asked: "Married or enjoying the swinging life of a Wild Game Hunter?"

"You mean the Big Bwana who lands in the arms of his female clients?"

"Well, it did cross my mind."

"Women go for that image. That's for sure!"

"I'd imagine."

"Yes, I suppose you do know all about that. Sure, I enjoy what happens, when it seems a good idea. But business is business. Don't like mixing things up. But if you're wondering, I'm not married. Was once...but that's a tired story. Have, since then, enjoyed the simple life of a Big Bwana. Good role. But, like I said, I try to keep hands off the clients. That's bad gaming."

"Isn't life all a game?" Bob nodded. He was beginning to feel little better about the safari. He liked Barton; this was a man who automatically inspired confidence.

"Not really. Its serious business that can end abruptly. So best to live to the hilt, as they say."

"That can be dangerous," Bob noted. Again the doubts needed him.

"Yes. But simply walking down a street can be dangerous. Death cowers at every corner to crush your life—like a fly being smashed. Life is too short." He paused, then added: "Guess you know that...read some of your books."

"Oh?" That startled Bob, but laughed it off with: "Hope they didn't shock you!"

"Well...truthful? You've colored things a bit here and there."

"I'm exposed! Coloring reality is the name of a writer's game."

John winked playfully at Bob. "Real or not, those books read like you've lived every bloody minute of them. Tell me, *are* they all that real?"

"Well," Bob decided to be vaguely honest, "not

everything. Author's license!"

"I suppose so. If you were to report some of the things I've seen, well, I don't think the general public would find it digestible, or commercial. I'd slant to public taste, too. Hell, we do it here. Make things seem more dangerous than they are. Come to Darkest Africa, face the savage beasts of the jungles with your bear hands and rip their hearts out!"

They both laughed at that.

Yes, Bob admitted, *I like this guy!*

"Really that bad?" he wanted to know.

"Hardly, but that gets customers!" he chuckled. "Gets their blood churning for blood-letting and adventure African-style! But I promise you thrills to delight the very center of your adventurous spirit!"

Bob decided not to react to that last statement. A part of him almost thrilled to the idea of what the next days offered.

The ground below was changing from yellowed open landscapes to jungle green. He marveled at the beauty of that view, stretching out to the very horizon where black clouds were starting to form.

As the sky darkened, the mood inside the plane changed, becoming abruptly quiet, as if everybody awaited some horrid force to shatter the illusion of safety.

The compartment door opened and Rita looked in, a concerned frown on her face. "Is everything okay?"

"Sure," Barton announced. "Just go back and enjoy the fun and games!"

"You planning on giving us a joy ride?" she snipped, almost angry sounding.

"Give the customers top bang for their dollars! Sure. Why not?" Barton laughed.

"That's not funny! I'll tell you when and where and what I want for thrills!" Rita snapped. Then with a sharp laugh turned to Bob, said: "Now isn't the right, hon?"

Bob was surprised by the sound of her voice. He merely nodded.

"Don't worry," Barton said, "nothing to be concerned about!"

"Better not be. I'm paying for safe trip. I don't want any complications!" she almost threatened. "Well, none I can't handle!"

Then she to Bob, "Having fun? And Games? Bet this is a thrill and a half for you!"

Her laughter was cutting as she slammed the door closed.

Barton noted: "Nice lady. You're welcomed to her!"

A deep gloomy atmosphere pressed down upon the four whites and five blacks in the plane. Silence and fear froze over them.

The woman's exit left a gloom over the two men. Bob felt uneasy about her continual mood changes.

Several times the plane jerked, as if slapped. At one point lightning flashed so close that sparks seem to fly across the wing.

Rita appeared again, this time savagely annoyed: "What's the hell's going on?"

Bob shook his head from side to side, grimly trying to give her silent warning. She squinted at him for a moment as if in confused thought, then shrugged,

"Okay, you boys handle things. You damned well, better!"

She slammed the door, again. This time nobody commented.

Barton, at the controls, had become tight lipped. The man kept looking at the instruments, which didn't seem to be reacting to anything. Several times he checked for weather reports. The silence in the plane only accented the silence in the world outside. Everything was waiting for the next explosion..

Then John whispered between tightly clamped teeth: "We might have to land somewhere...ride out the storm!"

"You kidding?"

"Nope." John Barton retorted softly.

"How much farther to where we're going?" Bob asked.

"About three hours! Assuming we can ride this out. That is."

Those words crushed in on Bob like a hammer. He couldn't speak and merely sat there aware of nothing but the fear eating up from his guts.

The radio suddenly crackled alive *"...turn back. Storm about to break in your area..."* It faded. Died.

Neither man said anything for a long time. The jungle was a mass of endless green below them. It moved snail-paced under the plane.

Then hell broke loose.

A flash of light blinded them, coming out of nowhere. The plane seemed to toss, almost spinning before John Barton managed to right it. The man was a wonder of control and skill in the manner in which he reacted.

Barton reached for the plane's radio mike and started speaking. It only took a few seconds to discover that the radio was totally dead.

For about twenty minutes more they continued to fly without conversation and then finally Barton turned to Bob and yelled, "I'm going to land!"

"Where?" The jungle seemed an endless carpet of dark green below them.

"Look at the sky—*landing is our only chance.*"

As if on cue, there was a flash of lightning and a split second later, the sound of crackling thunder.

Barton started dropping the nose of the plane.

"You can't land down there!" Bob cried.

"I'll have to find someplace!"

Suddenly the plane whipped to one side and at the same time lightning flashed and thunder sounded. Abruptly, it began to rain. There was a sick creaking sound from the body of the plane.

"Tell them—to strap in!" Barton ordered.

Without thinking, Bob slowly stood, trying to hold down the grind of fear cramping his stomach. He moved into the passenger compartment.

"Strap in!" he shouted. "We're going to land."

Rita started to say something, and then white-faced seemed to think better of it, and without a word doing as the man directed.

Bob was back in his seat a moment later, strapping himself in. Only then did he realize what he'd just done. He'd acted without thought. He wasn't even trembling.

Maybe he wasn't some raving cowardly shit!

Lightning flashed much too close, almost blinding them. The rain had become so heavy that they couldn't see much beyond a few hundred feet.

Suddenly the plane was whipped as if by some invisible giant hand, and the controls were useless against the gush of wind that followed. Bob felt the world spinning. Barton cursed loudly and after a few moments of fighting the plane, he managed to regain control. Just then, another lashing wind swept them sideways and then downward.

Bob was flung forward across the control panel. Then he was shoved savagely backwards, brutally hitting the seat with such force that his teeth jarred painfully together.

"Hold tight!" Barton warned. "Gonna...be bad!"

JUNGLE GODDESS, BY CHARLES NUETZEL

CHAPTER 3

Crashed

The zebra stood there in the jungle, its head bent down slightly, unaware of the danger lurking in the bushes at its side. The jungle was alive with the happy reassuring noises that brought no sense of fear to the animal. Suddenly, the jungle bushes rustled slightly as lightning broke through the branches. A nude female form leaped up onto the back of the animal.

Steel flashed in the sunlight as the zebra bolted across the clearing. The steel flashed again, coming out of the terrified animal with a blood-red point. The tiny female figure had her golden tan legs clamped tightly against the sides of the animal. Her body, browned from years of living under the hot, tropical African sun, was leaning forward. Her slender arms swung again, in a downwards arch, cutting deep into the neck of the frightened, bleeding animal. A high-pitched, excited sound broke from her young full lips as she jerked upwards, the sun highlighted the firm, full delicate outlines of her silken smooth flesh. She bent over once more, screaming in delight as the long, six-inch blade buried itself deep into the animal's neck. This time she left it in, pulling upwards with all her strength, so that the blade cut through the quivering flesh, slicing a long red streak. The zebra stumbled, reared and crumbled to the ground.

The young jungle savage jumped to her feet, looked down at the dead animal and then eagerly fell to her knees. She extended the knife outwards and sliding it into the flank, her lips spread into a broad smile and a tiny, delicate tongue moistened their surface as she cut away a large piece of dripping flesh.

Quickly placing the knife into the grass rope around her waist, she gripped the meat in her strong tiny hands and then brought it up to her mouth. Savagely she chewed on the bloody meal, her eyes flashing sideways, watching, waiting, listening for the approach of any jungle enemy. Every action was swift, but with a gracefulness that would have made the leopard look startlingly awkward. That was one of the traits that had let her survive in a savage world, where death was at every turn. She had always lived in the jungle. Or so it seemed, since memory offered little else but shadowy dreams to bother sleep. She knew little more than the laws of existence that the jungle had taught her.

Be faster than the others. Be smarter. Be more alert. And kill when necessary.

Beyond that there were merely those strange nightmares that haunted her dreams; visions of places totally alien, where white gods and goddesses seemed to rule a white world so different from the jungle in which she lived. Tallie had always wondered about the dreamland, for it almost seemed real in a vague way. But not as real as that which presented itself in full

30

consciousness.

Plus there was one basic truth of existence: you paid attention to the moment, for attention directed elsewhere was certain to bring quick death. Life had always been on a *now* basis.

A distant noise sounded in the sky and she looked up, startled. The sky was clear and her face relaxed. She returned her attention to the dripping, still warm, meat in her hands. Finally, when she was filled, she felt suddenly sleepy. She was always sleepy after eating. Lying down next to her kill and placing her head on its huge side, she went to sleep. Her senses remained alert and alive and ready to waken her at any possible threat of danger. Instinct and long experience prepared her for the approach of any animal eager to steal her kill. A warning snarl was usually enough to discourage any invasion of her territory—if that didn't work she would distanced herself quickly to a safer place. Like all the other jungle creatures, she never did more than half-sleep. Her mind rested, but her senses were still alert. Her body and muscles rested but not her ears and nose.

She lay there for a long time, resting contentedly, but subconsciously alert to the sounds around her. Then a flash of lightning startled her awake. Her eyes popped open and her heart started pounding wildly. She looked up fearfully.

Suddenly the sky started crying and her heart began beating in terror, her lovely, firm breasts heaving. She looked anxiously around her and then up at the sky once more. The first thought that passed through her primitive mind was that the gods were crying, but when the sound of thunder mixed with the flashes of lightning, she knew that it was much more than that. The gods were quite angry, spitting fire at her world.

Terror exploded in her heart and like a frightened wild animal she leaped to her feet, rushed for the nearest tree and started through the upper terraces of the jungle, swinging lightly from branch to branch.

The gods were at war, and when they fought, the very earth shook with terror and Tallie knew that the only way to be safe was to find the cover of her little cave. There, away from the crying tears of the goddesses as they wept in fear for their mates, she would be safe from the white fire-spears as they flew through the sky. Such spears of fire that could start the jungle roaring with heat and crackling with flame.

In minutes she had covered a quarter of a mile through the thick jungle, racing frantically to a cave not far away.

The roar of lions, the fearful screams of scampering monkeys and other jungle creatures surrounded her as all the animals cried out in their open terror.

Her breasts were hammering, throbbing with excited fear. She had seen many god-wars like this before and seen many horrible and terrible things happen because of the battles in the sky.

Finally, she reached a clearing and dropped to the ground, looking to all sides, ready for any unexpected attack, then rushed across the clearing and up to the small cliff side, following a narrow pathway and turning into the darkness of a shallow cave.

She sat down, her heart slowly regained its normal tempo. Finally, she looked up at the skies, fascinated by the gigantic war taking place there. Flashes of fire-spears fell from the sky as the roar of the gods moaned in death agonies. Then there was another sound, more puzzling than anything else. It was something new to the jungle, and only a whisper above the roar of the god-battle.

She looked skyward again, her bright blue eyes eager and alert. She brushed a long lock of golden blonde hair from her wide forehead, listened carefully. Suddenly a strange, huge bird covered the sky, just above the hill in front of her. It seemed to fall and then, roaring in terrible agony, it lurched sideways and then continued on for a while, then horrible sounds came as it dropped into distant trees.

An edge of interest showed on her delicate, lean features. Her full lips pouted slightly and she cocked her head to one side, listening.

What kind of bird could that be? she wondered. What strange new sky-animal had the winds brought with them?

She had lived for many, many seasons, longer than she'd ever been able to count on her fingers, but she had never seen such a sky-creature before.

Her heart beat faster, tightening inside her delicate chest, and curiosity welled wild in her savage mind. After the gods finish their battle, she would have to see what kind of sky-creature it was. Maybe a god! The thought excited her. Maybe a god that had been killed!

Her lips smiled and a sound, half squeal and half laughter broke from them. Then sighing, after looking once more at the sky, she curled up on the floor of the small cave.

There wasn't anything that she could do but

wait for the god-war to stop. Then she'd go out and see the "god creature" from the skies. Right now she was tired.

When sleep came, quickly, it brought ancient dreams back into existence. As if seen through thick fog she was aware of strange voices speaking words she could just barely understand.

"We're not...going to make it."

"What'll happen to her?"

A generous face of a Goddess looked down at Tallie, smiled. It was as if she were looking at herself, but much older. The face faded. The sound of screaming surrounded her, the dream shifted and she was in the belly of some strange monstrous creature, looking out through a hole in its side as the world below. It was like swinging through the trees without touching a branch. The dream shifted again, fading, refocusing and then fading again, until it turned completely dark as if by some inner will it was being shut down.

The ancient nightmare slept in its deeply contained mental cage deep inside her mind.

* * * * * * *

Rita Bentley was fighting raw fear.

Bob's command to strap in jarred her. From the moment she remained in a state of terror, hating herself for having arranged this trip. How silly. That dark side of her personality had neatly planned things. To what purpose other than to have another wild adventure. But not this! She didn't want to die. Dark Rita didn't care! That part of her lived on the cutting edge of life, as if death were an inviting option. And sometimes all of her simply wanted to toss in the towel.

Nobody spoke. The only sound was the plane moaning against the building storm outside.

She hated storms.

It had been on a stormy night that her mother, in a depressive state, had driven over a cliff—nobody thought it was an accident. Rita was thirteen at the time.

People said she was a lot like her mother. She remembered very little about the woman. In fact, much of her childhood memories were muddled, cloudy.

Lightning flashed, driving her attention once more to the almost blackening sky through which they were tumbling.

She felt out of control, helpless. And at such times the nasty Rita surfaced! This bitchy side had been taking over far more often in the last months. Pills helped. Confused, Rita couldn't remember if she'd taken one of them this morning.

Oh, shut up, and let me in! An unwanted voice said in her head. *I'll take over, and you can just sleep!*

Leave me alone! Rita pleaded, frantically looking for her handbag. The plane jerked violently. She couldn't find the purse. It wasn't there!

Give it up, dear Rita. Let me enjoy the fun and games. We always enjoy life better when I'm in control!

It wasn't even possible to debate the issue with her inner self.

After that things happened very fast. Lightning burst like flames in the sky, the plane lifted, plunge downwards. Rita's head hit something, and then she was bodily shoved backwards.

35

Darkness slammed consciousness away. Awareness came only in throbbing flashes with vague memories from the past. At first it was impossible to focus. Lurid images flashed through her mind.

A dark form leaned over her, a hand reach out, touching her naked breasts. A murmur of pleasure shivered along her spine, into her groin, as a soft voice said: "You're too lovely."

It was the drunken slurred voice of her father.

Rita's mind cleared only slightly.

She never knew if she was a victim of incest. Her father never touched a drop of liquor after that night.

She tried to push that memory away.

Rita was never really close to her father. No matter how hard he tried to bridge the gap with gifts and money. Dark Rita made sure of that.

She hated that side of herself! The bitchy Rita had been the cause of more tabloid attention than either of them wanted. Drinking, wild parties and a nasty relationship with the press helped feed the tabloids with headline stories about the rich Rita Bentley and her endless list of male lovers.

Yet those lies hurt—even when they were the truth.

Slowly the darkness ebbed away as she heard voices. It was some time before the words made sense. She was aware of moving, but it was as if her body acted on its own.

They'd crashed.

"Oh, God!" she moaned, eyes opening.

"Everybody seems to be okay," a voice said. That was John Barton.

36

She remembered some of it, now.

"You okay?" Bob asked.

She turned and saw the man sitting next to her on the ground. Beyond him was the dark shadowy ruins of the plane.

Somehow she'd gotten out of her seat, left the plane. Awareness ebbed back into place.

"Rita, are you okay?" Bob asked again, staring at her.

"I think so. Just a slight headache," she stated, somewhat puzzled by the calm numbing all feelings.

She saw Carol was stretched out on the ground, just a few yards away. "Is she–?"

"She's alive," the Bob assured her. "If that's what you mean."

JUNGLE GODDESS, BY CHARLES NUETZEL

CHAPTER 4

Doomed

Carol Hill slowly felt herself coming out of a long dark throbbing tunnel that had no light, at first.

"Carol—Carol, wake up!" a man's voice cried frantically, heavy with concern.

Finally, awareness started to get stronger, the throb continued, but light was beginning to brighten through her eyelids.

Oh, God, what happened?

Her eyes opened.

"What..." Carol stared up into the face of Bob Lake. He looked white, eyes narrowed, hard, as if struggling to contain his own desperate feelings.

"You're okay—keep calm," Bob instructed, helping her to a sitting position.

"We...crashed—" she moaned, abruptly remembering. Her eyes focused on the dark shape of the mangled plane some distance from where she was lying on the ground, surrounded by the others. For a moment the terrible reality of what had happened rammed in at her.

Carol felt completely dazed, shutting her eyes to blot out the images.

"We're okay. Just relax!" Barton instructed. "*All* of you."

At least everybody was alive, she realized. They should be dead!

It was several minutes before she could again open her eyes. Everybody was obviously unsettled, frightened. By then a numbed calm had settled over her nerves, washing the nausea away.

We haven't been killed...yet.

And who knew what the immediate future might bring.

The next minutes were a blur to Carol. She was aware of some things, but her own mind was struggling to deal with what faced them.

Somebody asked: "What happened?"

Barton announced, somewhat grimly: "We crashed. I couldn't avoid it. The storm has passed us, now. Don't know how long we were unconscious in the plane. But we're alive. That's what counts!"

"What now?" Bob's voice asked at one point.

Barton answered: "First thing is to set up camp and then discover what supplies we have left."

Rita cried, hysterically: "Oh, Christ! We'll *never* get out of this!"

"Sure we will," Barton assured her in a calm strong voice.

Carol's mind cleared a little and she looked up at Bob and extended her hand towards him. "Help me."

Rita might want to play the damsel in terror, but Carol wasn't about to feed into that game. Damned if she'd play the coward as long as they lived and had a fighting chance.

"You okay now?" Bob asked, as she stood.

"I think so. For a moment there, coming out of it, I was a little—but just think!" Carol exclaimed. Then, bravely, attempting to find some positive statement, said: "What a book you'll be able to do—*now! BOB LAKE LOST IN AFRICA!*"

Rita countered: "More like: *BOB LAKE DEAD IN AFRICA!*"

"Hey, cut that out!" Barton snapped.

The others looked a little dazed and uncertain.

Rita moved between Carol and Bob, thusly taking claim to her man.

John Barton surveyed the plane then said: "We best get started!"

Carol turned to the White Hunter, smiling. Her words were more confident sounding than she would have expected: "What can I do to help?"

The man instantly seemed satisfied that at least one of them was showing signs of outright courage and determination. "Sort out the things we'll be needing...just in case..."

Rita demanded: "Of what...?"

"We may have to walk back!" Barton stated, dryly.

Rita's quickly retorted. "*Walk*?"

It was as if the very word were some kind of perversion.

"I thought you were an adventurous lady," Barton offered with some humor.

"I'll walk a *mile* or so just for the *fun* of it," she admitted, "but this is *impossible*! Damned impossible!

41

I paid good money for your...*damn!* You can't get away with doing this to *me* and get paid for it, too! I *don't* pay for *failures*!"

They all looked at her, startled.

The white hunter shrugged: "If I fail, I suppose I'll never be able to cash your check. So stopped worrying!"

Bob soothed: "Easy does it, Rita! Things are bad enough!"

"Don't tell me what to do!" the woman snapped, nastily. "I paid this...*man* here...good money..."

"Money can't buy us out of this!" Bob observed. "Sad to say."

"It damn well better!" Suddenly Rita laughed at that, a sharp shift in mood that surprised the others. "Well, money rules the world! Doesn't it?"

"Not always," John Barton observed. "Jungle beasts don't value money!"

"Well all the beasts I know have!" Rita countered, obviously offering a different twist to the man's words. She seemed to be suddenly in more control. The change was welcomed while at the same time unnervingly abrupt, as was the sharp laugh that followed them.

"Come on, guys! Can't you take a little kidding?" she demanded. "Like the man said: we'll alive!"

Nobody replied, instead turning to John Barton who was already starting for the crippled plane. The wings were ripped and the body dented and scared. Amazingly the landing had been a "safe" one; regardless of the obvious damage. And none of them had been hurt; that was even more of a miracle. In minutes they discovered that most of the supplies were completely ruined. What was left were a couple of revolvers—for the men; parts of two tents; a little food, and ammunition for the guns. The rifles had been damaged.

Rita made a frantic search, muttering: "Damn, where's my purse!"

"Forget that—just the necessary things!" Barton instructed.

"Crap! Damned pills!"

"Important?" the hunter asked.

Rita's face reflected real concern, though she shrugged. "Guess not! Oh, well, so much for that, little girlie! I can always buy some more." She laughed a bit nervously, edgy. "Assuming we find a drug store before we all die!"

"Not out here," Bob noted under his breath.

Carol's first personal, professional, concern was the cameras. And it became obvious that all was lost for very little was left of her equipment. The cases had been smashed open and cameras and lenses were crushed beyond repair.

"Now what?" she demanded, looking horrified at the damaged equipment. Her eyes were moist with frustration.

John Barton quickly said: "Don't bother with all that. We have more important matters!"

Carol gasped, held down a sharp retort, and then reconsidered. The man was right.

"It really doesn't matter," Carol announced, deciding to be realistic.

Rita laughed, nastily: "Well, lady, looks like your little project to fame has been busted!"

43

"That's not funny," Bob pointed out with some sympathy.

"I suppose not," was Rita's only response.

John Barton snapped: "Enough quibbling!"

The woman's hands clawed, lips thinned to hard lines. "How dare you! Where'd you get you're balls to order me around?"

"Just cut the crap!" Barton snapped, angrily.

The harsh commanding bite of his words shocked the others to silence. Rita glared at him, then slowly relaxed.

"Whatever Big Bwana say!" she muttered a bit too sweetly.

Barton studied the woman then said: "We best make camp for the night. In the plane we should be safe enough! We can decide what to do tomorrow..."

"You said we have to walk out of Africa..." Rita retorted, nastily.

"Out of here, maybe. *If that's necessary.* I just want you all to understand the situation. There are other options."

"And what might they be?" Rita wanted to know.

"We need rest. Clear our heads. Talk about our options tomorrow! This won't be much different from setting up a safari camp!" Barton said those words in such a manner that it left no room for further exploration of the subject at this time. "First things first!"

Rita started to say something, but bit her lower lip and remained silent, joining the others in following the hunter's instructions and lead.

It took several hours to clear and sort things and get the camp ready for the night. The four black bearers helped to get the camp in order. Barton built a fire outside the plane and then went out to hunt with a couple of natives. Rita had become silent and withdrawn while they organized the camp. Barton returned with a small antelope. No sooner had he dragged the welcoming animal into their camp than Rita suddenly cried out in horror, pointing beyond him: "What's that?"

The bushes at the end of the small clearing moved and a lion stepped out, glaring at them.

* * * * * * *

The jungle girl awoke sometime after the storm stopped.

The dream still held in her mind. It contained that vague nightmare sense of reality remembered. White creatures like herself, hovering over her—Gods, giants in strange clothing. And the giant bird in which they were all in, whose stomach must certainly surround them...all of that held focus for but a moment. It was simply part of a continued night world, the dreamland which her mind visited when sleeping. She didn't like those dreams. She didn't like what wasn't understandable. She always wanted to understand and know—her quick mind was a greedy instrument that demanded to solve puzzles and learn. It was that part of her which had made it possible to survive all these years.

Tallie shook herself and then shattered the dreams away, as if they had never existed.

She was hungry. That was the first thought that passed through her savage mind. She remembered the

God-bird that had fallen from the skies. Her eyes scanned the heavens and then the jungle.

She stood there a moment longer, not moving, then abruptly swung down the pathway. Reaching the ground, she ran across the clearing and reached up to an overhanging branch. She swung easily through the trees, leaping from branch to branch. It didn't take her long to locate the place where the god-bird had fallen.

A shiver of excitement and awe trembled through her as she peered from the branches of a high tree at the wreckage below.

It surely wasn't of man. It wasn't of the jungle. It wasn't of the blacks. It was something alien and different.

Then her eyes went wide with alarm. There were creatures moving around the god-bird! She saw that they were white. They were like the blacks in shape, but like her in color. She hardly noted the blacks hunched like dark shadows in the background.

Thought of the natives sent anger through her. Most of the ones she knew were running through the jungle killing each other, fighting and warring and stupid!

But what were these white creatures all about? Obviously they were the blacks' masters.

Instinctively Tallie felt a kinship with them; they were like the dream gods of her sleep world.

Were they gods?

Or creatures like herself?

Confusion moved across her mind, and her pretty face frowned with concern, trying to reason out what she saw and what it might mean to her.

Abruptly she was aware of the scent of a lion.

Tallie was at once alert to the danger. The bushes moved at the other side of the clearing, and then one of the god-creatures screamed and the others turned toward the bushes. Two male god creatures stepped forward and pointed out their arms at the bushes as they parted, revealing the mangy form of an old lion.

Tallie sat where she was, wondering what they would do.

She heard loud, commanding sounds come from the god-creatures. The two females moved back of the men and then there was the sound of a terrible explosion in the air. Then another. With each sound the lion growled and moaned. He jerked lightly as if being hit by stones.

What god-magic was this?

The beast turned, whipping around, its tail shot straight out, the signal for the springing charge. At the same time there were yells from the two men who rushed in, pointing their arms out at the lion, as great flashing explosions sounded from the ends of their hands.

The lion turned its head toward the men and Tallie leaped on its back, at the same time drawing her knife and plunging it deep into its side.

The knife plunged again into the lion, deeper, this time true to its mark. The animal dropped forward into the grass.

She slid down from its back, looking at her kill, then her eyes flashed up at the other whites. Without so much as a moment's hesitation she leaped into the nearby tree, out of sight from these strange white creatures.

JUNGLE GODDESS, BY CHARLES NUETZEL

CHAPTER 5

First Night

Rita Bentley laid back on the blanket, looking up through the jungle trees, the half moon lighting the night with a dim glow, hardly aware of these images. Sleep was illusive. She wanted to blot out the nightmare that had descended on them. Her head still hurt where it had been bumped hard during the crash. The events of the day had shaken her to a raw edge of inner terror. And the continued ebbing power of Dark Rita was becoming harder to rebel, as it kept taking over by little nibbles.

The throbbing headache kept its rhythmic drumbeat in the back of her skull.

The memories flooded in, then faded, returned, and faded in confusing patterns.

She had been horrid to Carol. The woman was actually rather nice. Even if obsessed by driving ambition.

Hate her! Little bitch! She'll be after the men!

Rita fought down those unreasonable thoughts, trying to convince herself that they were baseless.

Carol Hill was not at all interested in Bob Lake.

She better not be! I'd tear the little whore's eyes out!

As to the white hunter, she could have the bully!

On the other hand, Big John Barton was one hunk. Be interesting to know what he was like under all those clothes.

Dark Rita wanted to surface.

Go away, drop dead! she inwardly moaned. *Can't think! Don't want her. I wish she'd just die!*

Bob Lake's voice interrupted her thoughts: "You okay?"

Slowly she opened her eyes, looked up. The man was standing over her.

"I think so," Rita said, sitting up. "Just that bump on the head! Not even a lump! But I'm pretty shaken by all this."

"All of us are." He glanced at the dead lion. "I still can't believe that...jungle girl! Who the hell is she? Where did she come from? Where'd she go? Just a little, frail savage killing it with a bloody knife! Incredible!"

"Yes..." she agreed, eyes focusing on Bob's handsome face.

Such a strange man, Rita realized. He was a nice guy, even if somewhat of a puzzle.

Months ago she had hired a detective to learn more about him. The report revealed little. Lake had grown up in a small town, come out of nowhere to begin selling "true life" adventures—without any evidence of having actually done the amazing things his books reported. He was either a master of deception, hiding his trails, or a fake. He was an intriguing mystery she wanted to unravel. And that's why she had organized this safari. Well, the nasty Rita part of herself, anyway, was responsible for all that. Yet it appealed to the totality of Rita. She simply found the man interesting; a puzzle to dominate.

The headache numbed slightly, but even dulled it was an open door through which Dark Rita could surface.

"…truly amazing, that," Bob was saying, his words flowing in and out, almost disconnected. "Wonder where she came from." She focused on his voice. "Barton was somewhat surprised. Said he'd heard of rumors of a jungle goddess' appearing out of no-where—but considered them local native tripe."

"I was thinking about her, too," Rita lied, as he sat down next to her. "Strange!"

"Breathtaking!" he said with a grim smile, eyes again noting the lion.

Rita glanced at him, then looked toward the fire where Carol was sitting talking to the White Hunter. "How's little Ms Ambitious doing?"

"Actually she's the only one that seems to be really excited."

"That figures," Rita snipped. "Pretty young blonde thing out to capture the world in her camera," Rita whispered, this time less hostile, hiding the sudden unreasoned fury tempting to surface.

"Well, she's has a pretty good rep!" Bob noted. "I have to hand her that."

"I bet!" She bit down an unspoken comment about men always finding such women desirable. The Dark Rita was too near the surface.

"She wants me to focus the book on the jungle

girl," Bob noted conversationally. "You know, it isn't a bad idea...if anybody ever believed it! And assuming that we can discover more about her...which is iffy at best."

They were both silent for a moment, but she noted how his eyes kept moving to Carol's form, high-lighted by the flickering fire.

The darkness inside her was welling up. When she spoke, the words formed without any conscious thought:

"She's attractive, isn't she?"

He merely continued to look at Carol.

"Bet you want to wrap her 'round your..."

The words faded, forced to silence by her better half.

"Can't deny that," Bob laughed, getting the full implication of that incomplete thought. He chuckled. "Most men would!"

"You're all animals in heat!"

Instantly she wanted to retract that.

Dark Rita was eating at the very edges of her skull.

Bob countered with: "Thought you like men that way!"

"You bastard!"

He looked hurt. "What'd I do?"

"Oh...nothing...sorry! I can be a terrible bitch, at times. But I just hate it when a man is so honest! Can't you lie a little? Make me feel I'm special?"

"You are," he admitted.

"But a bitch. Right?" she managed to laugh it off. "A friggin' bitch in heat!"

But Rita smiled as she touched his cheek with

soft fingertips.

"Sure, and one hell of an exciting one," he offered, agreeably. His eyes swept over her body to underscore the words.

"You sure can be a wicked man, Mister Bob Lake!" she laughed, eyes searching for somewhere to be alone with him.

She leaned closer to him and whispered: "Bob, let's get lost!"

"That we are!" he pointed out.

"I mean over there!" she tugged on his arm, glancing towards the plane. "Behind that…thing!" The emotion in her voice said it all.

And what Rita wanted, Rita got!

As the two of them stood, John Barton called: "No wandering off!"

"Just want some privacy!" Rita tossed off over her shoulder. "We'll be good. I promise!"

* * * * * * *

Carol was curled up in a warm blanket next to the fire, which was kept blazing by the natives. Barton had made a comfortable area for all of them to rest. Though the plane itself was also offered up as a safe "jungle motel" in waiting. The hunter sat with the blacks, near the fire.

She watched him highlighted by the campfire, moving restlessly from time to time. The two of them had enjoyed quite a strange conversation after Rita and Bob had disappeared for whatever private action they wanted to enjoy. It wasn't hard to know what privacy meant to them.

53

John Barton was quite an impressive man. Totally different from Bob Lake and for that matter, any man she had met in the civilized world. There was strength about him that attracted Carol.

When asked about himself, he'd merely said: "Well, been here all my life. A stint in the army, though, gave me a momentary blink at the outside world—but I came back to my homeland to take up hunting, which I'd done most of my life anyway. Not much to tell."

Then he'd stared at her for some time. A warm wave curled down her spine under his gaze. She felt stripped naked.

"You're some lady, Carol," he had told her in a low voice. "Admire your courage."

"I'm really not that...brave. Just a driving ambition to become somebody," she managed, eyes dropping away from his.

"Your are somebody. Rather nice, too. No man in your life?"

"No private life, really." She felt suddenly uneasy.

"Bet you've left a lotta hearts crushed!"

Carol shook her head. "I doubt that."

He chuckled, shrugged. "Well at least you're modest, if nothing else."

"Just driven!" Then without realizing what she was doing, Carol found herself mumbling scattered thoughts about her past, how she'd clawed her way up from being a nobody. How her father had been a dominating figure in the family, somewhat of a put down artist. "He continually knocked me for wanting to get a career."

54

"Old fashioned type?"

"Yep. I suppose. Get married, have children. Really back to the mid-nineteenth century type. Considering where we are now...Look where I've ended up! In a mid-jungle crisis without a camera to record events...assuming we get back alive."

"We will," he assured her in a somewhat startlingly harsh voice.

"How can you be so sure?"

"I can't, of course. Tomorrow could bring instant death to any human being on this planet. We never know when our lives will end. We can only live them from day to day. Hell, I don't know. But we will survive—I've been in far worse situations than this and managed to end up here with you...now that's something, isn't it?"

The man's eyes swept greedily over her, as if he were a savage beast in heat. Then a broad smile made a mockery of it all. "We're alive. And don't you forget it!"

"I'll do my best!" she managed, shaking off doubts. "This was suppose to be a really super break for me!"

"You career women really puzzle me! Women should want to be mothers and..."

"Hey not all women are good mothers!" she pointed out.

"Hey, that's the standard: get married and have children. That's the design that has kept homo-sapiens going for thousands of years."

"Well, these are modern times!" she countered, somewhat seriously. "Why shouldn't a woman have a career?"

"Because women are happier when they are do-ing what God meant them to do? Does that make sense?" There was a sharp tinge of amusement in his eyes. "Why should you want to beat your head against the world? Why not let the male bash his head in? En-joy the secure cave he offers up as home for you and the kiddies?"

"We aren't cavemen."

"What? Are you kidding? I don't believe you!" he chuckled. "Me no caveman?"

"Didn't you know that?" she actually laughed.

Strangely the words didn't annoy her at all.

"Cave man or not, why batter yourself when you can send the local attractive gorilla to deal with the outside world?"

"Gorilla?"

"Yes. Aren't we men just big stupid gorillas willing to fall on the spear to protect cave and kids, to say nothing about the female girl-rillas?"

"Not this lady, thank you! I ain't no girl-rilla! You can bet on that!"

"Well, tell me about yourself!" he offered. "Maybe you are different!"

"I'm different, all right." Carol wondered at her own strange thoughts. Then her eyes lifted, met his. "Well, Dad told me that a woman was meant to be a mother. Breed like a cow! God, I hated that!"

"Well, that's what the good book says. Me. Well, I'm a conflicted kind of gorilla-man! One side is traditional, placing women as baby-makers, caretakers and homemakers. The other side sees another picture. In the jungle you have she creatures that don't follow our Western social customs. Not all animals obey the male lead. I recognized that with…mixed feelings."

The man chuckled, then offered: "Well the world is full of all sorts!"

"I suppose," was her only response.

Maybe the immediate situation changed things momentarily. Survival was all that counted and this man was their ticket. And as Carol looked at his hard, chiseled features, she felt a mixture of attraction and irritation.

Geeze, she thought, *what's wrong with you? He's just a man!*

But from the way he openly assessed her, as a female, was almost embarrassing. That was somewhat frightening. The power of his brazen stare was more than unnerving for it blatantly stated that if he wanted more he'd take more.

More what? How dare him!

Yet a warm glow flowed throughout her body.

She was glad when he had turned and directed his attention elsewhere.

Laying there in the shadow of the crippled plane, she let her thoughts linger on his gaze and her own mixed response to it. She was hardly a virgin, but at the same time not like Rita!

Well, if he thinks otherwise he's in for a surprise!

Frustrated, she tried to turn her musings away from the Big White Bwana! It was all like a fantastic dream—or nightmare. She couldn't decide.

She closed her eyes, blotting out the image of the man. Her thoughts shifted to the young, bronze jungle girl who had all but killed the lion with nothing but a knife. She shivered every time she thought about that.

She wondered what kind of book Bob Lake could make of this woman. *Bob Lake and the Jungle Goddess.*

Bob had been rather lukewarm to that idea when she'd mentioned to him. But, of course, chances were they'd never live to learn more about the woman.

They might be dead by tomorrow.

A shiver rushed down her spine. Suddenly she wished it was possible to be enfolded in John Barton's strong arms and protected from the coming dangers sure to assault them in the next days.

She left that thought unfinished.

It was some time before sleep finally closed in around her troubled thoughts, giving her exhausted body the rest it needed.

CHAPTER 6

Lost in the Jungle

The chirping of birds was the first thing that Carol became aware of. Then came the sound of voices heatedly talking.

Bob Lake: "What now?"

Barton: "I think we should stay here...rescue is sure to come—in time."

Rita Bentley: "Are you kidding?"

Barton countered: "Last night you seemed to think that was a good idea."

"Well, I've decided differently!"

"You women can never make up your minds!" Barton exploded, shrugging helplessly.

"Today is today. Maybe walking isn't such a bad idea. How would anybody know what's happened to us?"

Bob nodded: "Rita has a point. What would be our chances of getting out of here—walking our way out?"

Carol sat up, stood. She was somewhat puzzled by Rita's blunt shifting of attitudes, from no walk to all walk. It was as if the woman were two different people.

Rita pointed out: "We can't stay here! How in the world would they find us?"

Barton said: "I want to be bluntly honest: it's a fifty-fifty chance that they'll not miss us for a couple of days—and then it'll take many days—possibly weeks—before they find the plane crash. Or could be tomorrow."

Carol said: "Let's get out of here. A civilized outpost can't really be far!"

Barton nodded to that. "Okay—if the rest of you believe that's best..." But he sounded uncertain.

"Yes," Bob and Rita announced together.

"Okay, then, we might as well get things moving!" Barton said.

It didn't take long for Carol to gather her belongings together. They ate some of the meat from the animal John Barton had killed. Then they started gathering supplies and organizing things.

"I believe going northeast would be the best bet!" Barton suggested. "Find a river and then follow it to the coast. Or if I can get into territory I know, it'll be a lot easier."

There was a game trail which they followed for a short time, then one of the natives started taking the lead, cutting a path in front of them with his machete. Hours passed and Carol felt the hot tropical sun burn down on her. She was more than happy when the first break in the trek came and they could rest.

She stepped up to Barton and asked: "How many days, do you think?"

"That depends, Carol," he told her. "If we have

an easy run, with nothing getting in our way—maybe a week. Maybe sooner." He shrugged helplessly. "I want to be blunt, but not scary. I think we might as well get started again. It's going to be dark in a few hours and we have to cover as much ground as possible."

"Can't we find some place where we can take a bath?" Carol pleaded.

"I hope so. This territory is just as foreign to me as it is to you."

For what seemed hours they continued, sometimes taking game trails and other times cutting their way through the underbrush. Finally Barton called a halt in a small clearing. "This is just as good a place as any," he announced. "The first thing to do is to attempt to mend the two tents into one, build a camp fire and see what kind of foods might be gathered for dinner."

The natives fixed the tents, which worked out fine. They all crashed early.

But Carol didn't sleep well, half dreaming, half thinking. Several times the image of John Barton would come before her, tall, muscular, eyes literally stripping her naked, feasting on her flesh, almost caressing it and then she was aware of his hands as they reached for her, pulling her against his body.

Sleep vanished and the dream played teasing games with her mind. She thanked the "gods" that nobody could read her mind! But the dream was her own fantasy; and how delightful, delicious. Irritated she shook that thought away. This was hardly the time for foolish, little girl sexual fantasies.

Finally Carol slipped from under the blanket and quietly stepped out of the tent and looked around at the small camp. She wondered if they would ever really get out of this alive. A little walk was what she needed, but she didn't like the idea of going into the jungle alone. Barton had cautioned against wandering from camp.

Sighing, Carol took out a pack of cigarettes and lighted one, taking a deep puff. She normally didn't smoke, but right now desperately needed something to lean on. She felt at loose ends, needed to get away, think, try to sort her thoughts. She started moving toward the edge of the clearing.

"Where are you going?" a voice asked from the darkness.

Startled, Carol turned. "Oh, Bob, you frightened me. I thought everybody was asleep."

"You shouldn't be wandering around in the night like this."

"Why not?" she asked, an edge of irritation in her voice.

"It's not safe."

"I just want to take a walk, that's all."

"Into the jungle?" he asked.

"What makes you think I was going—?"

"I was watching you from the moment you stepped from the tent." Bob moved a little nearer to Carol.

She said: "Well, now that you're with me, why not come along?"

"Barton told us—"

"If you're frightened," Carol interrupted, tauntingly, somewhat peeved by her attitude towards the man. "You can stay!"

She started through the underbrush. All of a sudden it wasn't a point of taking a walk, it was a point of doing something that somebody had told her not to do. She had always rebelled from domination. That was her father's fault. He'd dominated the family and his wife and two children to the point of misman-agement. Life with father hadn't been nice—he'd never amounted to much, other than being a heavy drinker and office manager. He would disappear for days at a time, on a drunken binge. Her mother did more to support the family as a waitress. A couple of times the man had devoured her developing teenage body as if he wanted to do far more than stare.

She shook those thoughts away.

Carol hadn't gone more than seven yards when she heard Bob rushing after her.

"Don't be a little fool!" he hissed, anxiously.

"Oh, be quiet and come along if you want. I need a walk."

"After today's little walk?"

"This is different!"

Bob was stepping up beside Carol now and his hand reached for her arm, stopping her. "Look --"

"Please, Bob!" Carol stared coldly into his eyes. Her expression was firm and set. "Either stop arguing or go back to camp!"

The man looked at her for a moment and then sighed. "Okay, we'll walk. But not far. Not beyond sight of the camp!"

For a few moments they walked in silence and then Carol paused and turned towards Bob. "I can't understand you."

"What does that mean?"

"Oh, everything. Well, what I really mean is that I can't understand your drinking. I mean that...I'm sorry, none of my business.... I mean...well, hell! Forget it."

Angrily Carol stomped off, confused by her own actions and her own words. She didn't really know what she had been trying to say.

"Wait!" he ordered, his face showing grim outlines in the dim moonlight.

She stared at him, for but a moment, then said: "If you want to join me, fine."

They started off again, in silence for a few moments. Then Bob said: "You know, we've been friends for some time and you pointed out something that I guess I'd never thought much about before...that we hardly really even know each other. A shame, really."

Looking into Bob's eyes suddenly made Carol feel uncomfortable, nervous. There was something about Bob Lake, regardless of what kind of a man he was, that attracted her. Not in a romantic nor sexual way. But he reminded Carol of her brother Jack who had been a boozer, too, a dreamer lost in a fog of indecision. It had killed him in the end.

Her brother had wanted to be an artist—but never made it beyond selling a few painting for pennies. Maybe that was what she felt in her connection with Lake.

For fifteen minutes they walked, moving through the underbrush. Then Bob suddenly blurted out: "Are you sure we're going in the right direction?"

"Of course," Carol assured him in a weak voice.

They continued walking, in silence. But with every step, Carol had the terrible feeling they were going in the wrong direction.

Finally she stopped.

"Maybe it was off in this direction," Bob suggested, pointing to the left. "I'm sure that we circled...I mean this looks familiar."

Bob took only one step and then was stopped by the terrifying moan of a lion.

The lion looked at them, its eyes fiery, and then it moved through the bushes, not more than three yards from them.

Suddenly Carol felt weak, her knees were beginning to tremble. The world was just about to cloud in around her when she saw the blurry form of Bob Lake sink to the ground.

God! I can't pass out, now! she thought frantically. *Geeze, some adventure hero the mighty Mister Lake was!*

With a will that Carol hadn't known she possessed, she forced awareness back into focus.

It took several minutes before the man showed signs of coming out of it. First he moaned and then his eyes fluttered and opened.

"Come on, Bob...everything's okay." Carol couldn't keep the contempt from her voice. It was simply impossible; a woman could do such a thing— but not a man. Barton wouldn't have passed out.

After a couple of minutes Bob sat up and looked at her. "God, that was close...I don't know what happened. All at once I blacked out."

"Nervous reaction!"

Sighing he said in a weak, tortured voice: "I'm sorry."

"Forget it," Carol told him, feeling sorry for the man.

"I hope you'll keep this...well, not tell—"

"Our secret," she promised generously, realizing the implications of his request. "The thing we have to do is get to camp—and fast! The night jungle is too dangerous."

"Let's!" Bob stood and she followed him.

They started off deeply wrapped in tormented anxieties. It was some time before they realized they had taken the wrong direction.

"We've either passed it or are..." Bob let the words fade out, as if terrified to finish the sentence.

Carol bit her lower lip, feeling a sick panic push through her stomach. "Let's face it, Bob. We're lost!"

* * * * * *

Tallie had been watching the whites from the moment they left the god-bird. She had watched silently and unseen, from the trees. She couldn't help wondering what had caused the noise and flame to shoot out of the white's arms. She decided to watch and wait and see what happened. Only when she was hungry did she leave them to find food. From the direction in which they were going, she knew they were heading right towards the local blacks' village.

Tallie heard one of the men and one of the women talking and then the pair had started out into the jungle. She couldn't help wondering where they were going, or why. When the lion stepped across their path Tallie was ready to spring down upon it at the first sign that the animal might charge. Then the man fell to the ground and the woman rushed to his side.

Tallie felt sudden contempt for the man. The woman showed courage. She watched in silence while the woman revived him. The two stood and talked. Then started off, moving away from their camp again.

What Tallie had guessed before, she knew to be true, now. The whites were lost.

Quickly she rushed through the trees, ahead of the two below her, moving from branch to branch and then swung down to the ground.

JUNGLE GODDESS, BY CHARLES NUETZEL

CHAPTER 7

Captured

John Barton suddenly woke. It was as if some subconscious mental finger had jarred his mind from sleep.

It was still dark.

What had caused him to wake?

Barton's eyes moved around the camp, searching. The first thing that he spotted was the blanket Bob Lake had been sleeping in. His eyes scanned the ground and followed the fresh prints that led toward the jungle edge.

"Bob! Hey Bob!" he shouted. "Bob!"

"Say, what's going on?" Rita Bentley's voice called from the tent.

"Nothing for you to worry about!" Barton yelled back.

"Is Carol out there with you?"

"Oh, Goddamned. Those bloody fools!"

The only thing to do was to fire a shot in the air. If they were lost they would hear it and that would give them direction.

Rita Bentley stepped up beside Barton. "Where's Bob?"

"I don't know. He and Miss Hill took off for— no doubt a walk. They might be lost. They didn't answer my call. Maybe the sound of a gun shot would...it's the only thing we can do, right now, any way!"

"I just *bet* they went for a *walk*!" Rita snapped nastily. Her hands clawed into little fists. "I'll fix her."

Barton was a little surprised, but merely turned to glance at her. "Look, this can be serious. Personal feelings be damn! If they went for a walk, or just be alone together—if we get them back unharmed, you better not start a scene! The next days are going to be hard enough without that..."

"*I'll* do as I *damn* please."

"Not while I'm in charge," he snapped, pulling the revolver from his holster.

Startled, she backed off: "Don't you *dare* threaten *me*!"

He laughed coldly, said: "Wouldn't think of it!" and aimed the gun toward the sky He squeezed the trigger. The explosion was like a canon, bursting on the night air.

"What the hell!" Rita asked in a tight voice.

"Hopefully they'll hear that. But I can't just wait for them..." Barton turned toward the natives who had been standing beside him. "Could you follow tracks in the night?"

The tall, elderly headman stepped up to Barton and said in a low voice: "Yes, Bwana."

The man knelt down to the ground. "This way,

Bwana!"

They followed. Barton started to tell Rita to stay in the camp, but decided to let the matter go. It would mean an argument with a bitchy strong-headed woman. He figured to only fight the battles he could win.

They moved through the dark jungle for about fifteen minutes, circling and doubling back and circling again, but always away from the camp.

Then suddenly all three were startled by the sound of drums. They froze. The muscles on Barton's face tightened.

"What's that?" Rita cried in alarm, stepping in front of the tense Barton.

"Trouble," was his simple answer.

"What did the drums—?"

"Just that we're not alone!—the gunshots probably triggered this off. They don't like strangers...best to find Bob and Carol—fast!"

"1 thought they weren't any more savages in Africa!" Rita gasped in real alarm.

"Honey, there aren't many places like this left in Africa...but this is one of the few nasty spots!"

They hadn't gone more than ten minutes further into the jungle night than when suddenly they were surrounded by a band of savage natives, holding spears, which instantly threatened them.

Rita screamed in open terror.

For a moment John Barton started to consider alternatives, but the natives instantly swarmed in close and overpowered him.

* * * * * * *

71

Carol looked at the jungle girl, her mind startled and her body frozen with surprise. Where had she come from?

"What the damned hell!" Bob Lake shouted in surprise.

For only a moment were they able to just stare in amazement. The jungle girl motioned to them to follow her.

That's when they heard the gun shot.

"What's that?" Carol demanded, her throat constricting in terror.

"Come on, let's get the hell out of here!" Bob shouted.

The jungle girl moved toward them, her face gesturing, trying to communicate. Her delicate hand and arm motioned to them and then she started pointing to their right.

"She's trying to lead us somewhere!" Bob observed, his voice tight and high pitched.

"What're we going to do?" Carol whispered in Bob's ear.

"Follow her, I guess. There's nothing else we can do!"

The drums started then, and a wave of terror shot through her. That decided Carol. She started off after the jungle girl.

For a long time they followed the girl through the underbrush, neither of them saying anything, but concerned with their own fears and doubts.

They walked for over thirty minutes before the woman motioned the two to come to a stop. She listened for a moment and then started forward again.

They followed and in a few minutes they came to a clearing and Carol recognized it as their camp site.

Her heart beat faster with joy and she turned to look at Bob. "I didn't think we'd be seeing it for— Where'd she go?"

The naked girl had suddenly disappeared.

For several seconds they looked at each other in puzzlement. "I wonder if the others are still asleep?" Carol said.

The natives were awake, standing around the now large fire, murmuring and flashing their shiny bright eyes around at the jungle surrounding them. Normally they looked amazingly intelligent, wise to their own world and self-assured as to how to survive in it. But right now they seemed to be quite unsettled.

Neither Barton nor Rita was anywhere to be seen.

"What ever happened to them?" Carol cried. "They aren't here."

"Where's Bwana Barton?" Bob asked, moving toward the natives.

The two startled natives turned and stared at Bob. One of them stepped boldly forward and announced: "They look for you, Bwana Lake. They look for you!"

* * * * * * *

Bob felt a sickness within him as he pulled out a pack of cigarettes and offered one to Carol. But the fear that had so terrified him in the jungle slowly ebbed away. In fact, even that fear had been strangely different than he might have imagined it to be. The aftermath feelings were mixed. One part of him thrilled to their survival; another side shivered at what they'd been through. Yet they were still living and breathing; they'd survived. They were safe in camp; Barton should be able to take care of himself.

Bob stepped up to the fire, trying to find some warmth there to take the chill from his bones. But the chill was caused by something more than the cold air; it was an icy shiver that worked its way down his spine.

How could a man be such a damned coward? he wondered. *Yet at the same time feel a tingling sense of...what? Pride at survival?*

He didn't doubt that experience could be a harsh teacher. But how much could it actually change a man? Could an outright coward become something less horrid?

His life had been filled with running, turning away from reality. As a young boy he had read adventure novels until they came out of his ears. In his teens, women had been something to be frightened of—and he'd put his nose in another book. Not until he was in college did he know what it was like to possess a woman. Now he was known throughout the English-speaking world as a man with guts and courage, who could fight against all kinds of impossible odds in his search for adventure.

Carol Hill probably knew what he really was: a bloody chicken cowardly fake!

As he sat there agonized with self-guilt and shame, the soft rustle of foliage sounded from behind him.

He heard the sound, but dismissed it as the normal night jungle noises.

Then suddenly, hands grabbed hold of him.

Panic set in.

The first thing Bob knew was that he was facing a savage black face.

Bob struggled only long enough to realize a dozen natives, clothed only in lion cloth, armed with primitive spears and knives, surrounded him.

Then he shouted: "Carol—Carol...run!"

If only he had his gun, he thought, totally ignoring the fact he had never killed a man in his life—not even an animal.

Something struck him in the mouth—it was a hard object that brutally tore at his flesh, breaking the skin against his teeth.

The three black bearers came to their feet, saw what was happening and started to offer defense. But the invader quickly surged over them. In moments they were dead.

One of the natives stormed into the tent and Bob heard a scream, then silence.

A moment later the native returned, pushing Carol in front of him. Her face was white, her eyes large and frightened. It was the first time Bob had seen her so shaken.

He felt a surge of anger and strength tear at his muscles. The sight of Carol being pushed by the savage, the fear in her face, had snapped something within Bob. A foggy madness surged in around him like an invisible blanket, smothering all sanity. He strained with every muscle. His arms jerked free from the man holding him and he leaped toward the native who now gripped Carol in strong large hands.

Bob smashed into the black man, the weight of his whole body slamming the man down onto the ground. Bob fell on the man, his fists swinging, vision red and hazed with rage. He felt hands grab him, then something hit the back of his head, but he kept swinging until another sharp blow at the base of his skull brought a curtain down over his consciousness.

* * * * * * *

Carol felt herself being pushed through the jungle night but was only half aware of her surroundings. For the first time in her life she was really frightened. The sudden death of the bearers and then what followed stunned her.

The way Bob Lake had charged at the native holding her, beating the man senseless before the others had been able to stop him, left her breathless, amazed.

The last person in the world to do such a thing would have been Bob Lake. It left Carol dazed with surprise. Another emotion had flooded through her when she'd seen Bob fall unconscious to the jungle floor. She'd been sure he was dead. Then, when she saw the natives lift him, and one carry Bob on his shoulders, she knew that he must be alive.

She thanked God for his survival; then wondered for what purpose he had been saved.

What was going to happen to them? The very thought chilled her. Her mind imagined all sorts of horrors, including becoming a sexual slave to these men. That idea sent a chill through her. Carol felt that a quick death would be much easier to face. Yet she wasn't about to give up hope!

* * * * * * *

The sun was just beginning to show signs of rising over the horizon when they came to a clearing in the jungle which was crowded with grass huts, surrounded by scores of natives.

The women, naked from the waist up, looked at the small party that came out of the jungle. One of the natives in the party with her said something, shouting at the women. They stepped away, muttering angrily between themselves.

The men in the village watched Carol as if she were some delicate, delicious prize. The expressions on their faces beamed, their white teeth grinned at her as their gaze covered her body with savagely anxious eyes.

A shudder rushed over her as she was pushed through the village, past dirt smeared grass huts.

The man carrying Bob Lake finally came up beside Carol

As they all came to a stop in front of a small, vile smelling hut somebody pushed Carol from behind toward the small entrance. The implication was obvious.

Carol stepped forward, bent down and walked into the small confines of the hut, followed by the man carrying Bob.

The writer was roughly thrown on the floor and the native gave his ribs a cruel, brutal kick, and then walked out.

A guard was placed in front of the hut.

Trembling, sick inside, tears beginning to well in her eyes, Carol slipped to the floor, huddled against her knees, wondering why she was there, what had driven her all these years simply to end here—for the rest of her life. Some Big Break this had turned into. Suddenly the idea of becoming a famous photographer dimmed against the mere idea of getting back to civilization, alive and in one piece. Fat chance, was all her mind could conclude.

Well, Miss Hill, looks like your life long dreams have turned somewhat sour!

It was a long time before she had the strength or will to think about Bob Lake, and even longer before she cared enough to attempt to revive him.

All she could think of was the fact that death faced her; a death that she'd do anything to escape from—anything but allow her body to be used as a plaything for the men of the village. Carol knew that somehow she was either going to die, by her own hand, or find some means of escape—which she feared was impossible!

One part of her rebelled from such defeatist thoughts; she was still alive and had survived this far.

But for the moment she would wait, keep alert to any chance to escape or, at least, survive long enough to...find a way out of this horrid fate. Somehow.

* * * * * * *

Tallie had swung off into the jungle after having taken the whites to their camp. A strange feeling had settled over her while in the presence of the man; what it was she didn't understand but it was most unsettling.

It was just beginning to get light, the day God was coming out of his den of rest.

Tallie peered down through the branches just in time to see a group of blacks walking along the game trail, pushing two whites in front of them. At first she thought they were the two she had returned to the camp, then she saw they were the other two whites.

She looked at the tall, strong white hunter, admiring his carriage and stance. When a native prodded him with a spear point he acted as if nothing had touched him.

The woman was cowering and cried out in terror every time a native touched her.

More interested in watching the whites than anything else, Tallie followed in the trees above them, admiring the man and ignoring the woman.

She followed the small group until they came to the clearing and village of the blacks. She sat on a tree branch, hidden in the foliage, watching as the two whites were shoved into a small hut. For a long time she sat there. She couldn't understand why they had allowed the blacks to capture them, why they had not spit fire from their hands. Maybe the lightning didn't work against humans—maybe it only worked against the jungle creatures.

Standing, Tallie moved off through the branches, almost forgetting about the whites and their fate in her search to satisfy the craving of her hunger. Maybe after that she would return to the village and see what happened. In the meantime, Tallie decided to return to her cave and get the bow and arrows she had made. After having watched the natives she had learned how to make arrows and bows and how to use them, and perfected her ability with this modern—to her—weapon.

CHAPTER 8

A Daring Escape

John Barton quickly searched his surroundings, discovering there was no way out of the hut other than the opening, in front of which stood a guard.

Rita was huddled in the middle of the hut, sobbing almost hysterically.

"Shut up!" John snapped annoyed. "That won't get you anywhere!"

He stepped to the young woman and gripped her shoulders, shaking her. "Rita! Snap out of it!" John raised his hand and slapped her across the face. It was a hard, stinging blow and cut off the sobs as if he had turned off a radio.

For a moment Rita Bentley looked up at him and then suddenly buried her face against his chest.

"Look, there's nothing we can do right now— but we're alive." The moment he said that, John realized it was a mistake.

"For how long?" Rita managed to whisper between trembling lips.

"I ain't dead....yet!" he stated with a determined

smile on his lips. "You can't toss in the towel...and you can't let fear get in the way of sound action! We'll get our chance—then make our move!" He sounded even convincing to himself; only a silent, inner voice admitted to any sense of doubt.

She clung tighter to him, as if seeking comfort and some kind of control over her terror.

For the first time John felt a temptation which was almost overwhelming. Chances were they wouldn't live out the next week—possibly the next day; perhaps not even the next hour. In the face of death things seemed completely different.

"We aren't going to live—are we?" Rita inquired in a trembling voice.

John felt it was more humane to tell her that they wouldn't live rather than the truth about what would happen to her after the savages had gotten rid of him. As a white woman in the hands of savages she'd live out her life as a plaything for the males of the tribe, until she became pregnant, at which time the men would play a game that was even more than cruel. No, he thought, it was much more decent to say nothing or that they would both be dead in a short time.

She trembled against him.

John knew instinctively that in time Rita would make the first movements at seduction; for she was that kind of woman. In fact, it was quite human to seek escape if even for just a moment—hiding from the horror in an instant of brutalizing passion. They were in the same boat, so to speak, and only their fate would be different. He'd be brutally killed—a far less frightening end for it would come quick enough.

82

* * * * * * *

The first thing Bob Lake knew was being cradled against a woman's breasts. Immediately he thought it nothing but illusion. Then as he heard Carol's soft controlled voice murmuring, he knew it had been the truth.

The semidarkness gave just enough light to see Carol's features dimly outlined against the gloom. He could just make out moisture in her bright eyes and realized she had been crying.

Sitting up, Bob surveyed his surroundings and immediately guessed where they were. Strangely enough, he wasn't as frightened as he might have imagined under such circumstances.

"How long have we been here?" was his first, coldly controlled statement.

Carol blinked and stared at him for a moment before answering. "Not long," she told him in a shaky voice.

Bob nodded. "How long has it been light out?"

"About an hour." Then suddenly she blurted: "Bob...they're going to kill us!"

He hesitated, uncertain what to do, say. The reality of those words sank in like lead yet, strangely, had no personal meaning to him.

Bob moved to her, placed a protective arm around her shoulder. He was on the verge of pulling her into his arms when a tall native stepped into the hut, grabbed hold of Carol.

Bob was just about to leap into an attack when another couple of natives pushed past the first and grabbed hold of his arms, holding him back.

The first native, whose headdress was different from the rest, covered with bright colored feathers, gripped hold of Carol's blouse. A leering grin played on his thick lips as he brutally tore it from her.

Carol screamed a loud piercing cry of terror. Then she suddenly went limp, unconscious.

* * * * * * *

Tallie had gone to her cave, picked up her bow and then started down a game trail. Her thoughts turned back to the whites and then she remembered that she'd left the first two at their campsite.

Tallie quickly changed direction and started toward the campsite. When she arrived at the camp, slipping down out of the trees, she quickly interpreted the information so vividly written there. The dead bodies of the three natives told her pretty much what had happened. She searched the strange object next to the cold fire. It was a skin cave, she concluded after having gone inside. It was much like the grass caves in which the natives lived.

After having satisfied herself that nobody was in camp and that chances were the two had been captured as well, Tallie headed toward the native village.

* * * * * * *

When John Barton heard the feminine scream, he was sure it must be Carol Hill. Rita froze at the sound and a tremble shot through her.

"What was it?" she whispered. He felt her body arch up more tightly against his own, soft, sensual, inviting, as if desperately seeking comfort, protection, strength.

John didn't say anything; he merely listened. *If that were Carol and....* He hated to even think about that. The thought kept circling in his brain, over and over again. He pictured Carol dead, or worse, in the hands of the natives! The mental pictures that kept building in his brain created a hard lump in his throat.

The silence that followed was horrifying.

Then he became aware of Rita's body, warm, alive, trembling against his. It was a desperate plea, a demanding act of almost insane need—selfish and all enveloping.

The terror had drove Rita's body into a raging fit of passion. She arched up against his. She moaned as her body captured him deeply within it, demanding, unrelentingly demanding.

* * * * * * *

Bob somehow twisted free of one of the men holding him. Without thinking, like a man gone insane, he swung a fist into the gut of the second man holding his left arm.

Not waiting to see the effect of his blow, he leaped at the man who had attacked Carol Hill. All the pent up fears of a lifetime were smothered in the wild rage that suddenly surfaced under the pressure of the moment. He'd never faced real danger before, never been driven to a point where killing action might be demanded. Only in books and then in writing, had Bob Lake imagined such scenes. Now, in the last hours, for the first time in his life, he was experiencing a new self-awareness—he didn't even have time to consider the obvious change.

The killing instinct which is always just below the surface of all men soared powerfully through Bob's every nerve and muscle. All he could think of was battering this man who had dared to touch Carol. It didn't occur to him that what he was doing was pure madness. That he could kill the man before being overpowered by the others didn't enter his mind. He wasn't a fighting man; this was a trained warrior, a primitive used to killing. But rational thought was stripped from his mind. Something snapped inside at seeing the man strip the blouse from Carol's body. He felt an uncontrollable hatred, a driving need to kill. All the life long self-disgust surfaced in an overwhelming wave of rage.

The native's eyes were bulging from their sockets by the time the other natives managed to get hold of Bob. It took their combined strength to pull him off their chief.

Bob fought like a madman, swinging from left to right, hitting, kicking, in an insane attempt to go back to killing the chief.

The next thing he knew was that two men were dragging him across the small clearing in the middle of the village. Men, women and children were crowding around, laughing gaily as if they were expecting some sort of exciting show.

Groggily, he was aware of the two husky natives rushing him forward, knowing that it was only a matter of minutes before he would be dead. It was well for him that he wasn't aware of exactly what the enraged tribal chief planned—for it would be many hours before they would let him die. For the moment all he could think of was the amazing release that rushed through him at the surge of rage he'd experienced. No fear; just the killing instinct rushing to the surface—no thought of anything else had existed in that moment when his fingers were choking at the very life of the bastard's throat. The surge of inner power, mixed with the stunningly unexpected thrill of having overcome his natural sense of fear, blocked all other sensations.

Maybe I'm not such a coward, he rationalized with insane conviction. What he'd done was much the same as how he would have chosen to write that very scene—action without thought of personal danger. The "fictional" Bob Lake had for a moment become a reality. Only later would he begin to entertain doubts.

Bob was brutally tied to a tall, strong post that had been in the middle of the clearing for as long as the village had existed. The ropes, which bound his flesh, were tight, bursting, cutting at the circulation in his wrists. The natives had stripped him from the waist up and now the chief, whom Bob had attempted to kill, stepped up in front of him, face leering into a contorted grin of satisfaction. He spat out something at Bob and then pulled a small knife from his loincloth.

Until only a few moments before, Bob had never been a brave man, but what had just happened revealed another side of him. Perhaps it had always been there, hidden, just waiting for the moment to surface. Maybe imagination was a fantasy projection of what a person would, in reality, do when faced with real danger. Who knew? Only in fictionalized articles and books had it been hinted at. Right now Bob Lake had no time to consider such rationalizations. When faced with the right cause, Bob could and would fight, without considering any danger to himself. That fact was stunning to him; and he clung to it in this moment of self-realization. It was all he had to hold to against what must certainly now follow.

If his new conviction was madness, so be it. At least it was better than shivering and trembling in raw terror. Bob realized something about himself and possibly about the whole human race. One has their breaking point and their moment of courage. His thoughts raged from amazement and fear and then a sense of inner peace, and back again to the horror of what was taking a place. At the same time there was a sense of pride: facing death, now, he would gladly have died to save Carol Hill.

The knife point gleamed as the man reached out toward Bob's chest. The chief pressed the knife under Bob's chin, pricking the flesh.

For a moment Bob looked at what he knew was death and a tremble of fear and terror overwhelmed all thought. The old, life-long terrors rushed in to drown the new-found confidence that had driven him for a few minutes. It was as if all the energy had been drained away, leaving an empty shell to face his immediate fate. The momentary calm disappeared, shuddered away, and suddenly he was screaming, straining against the tight bounds that held him against the thick pole.

Maybe if he screamed loud enough some supernatural power would come to his aid; or insanity would give escape from reality. Maybe if he screamed long enough the nightmare would shatter.

And so he screamed almost in delight while at

the same time hating himself for screaming.

God, this can't be happening, a part of his mind cried out, welling up inside of him, attempting to block out reality. But unlike when creating such a fiction scene he couldn't edit or change or cut what was about to take place. He was helplessly caught in a nightmare reality from which there was no escape.

And so he screamed in the insane hope that this mere sound would somehow give escape—make reality disappear and fantasy replace the terrible end that now faced him. He screamed in manner of a madman desperately hoping the sound could drown the coming physical pain that was destined to torture his body in its last moment of existence.

All he could think of was that he would die for no good purpose. His whole life a mockery; wasted in fantasy. And Carol would be left to the savage lust and lecherous satisfaction of the men of the tribe.

* * * * * * *

John Barton was just sliding away from Rita when he heard the scream. What had just taken place between the two of them both annoyed and disgusted him. Not that the woman was undesirable, only that her greedy demands were overwhelming. He was, also, angry at understanding, to some extent, what had driven her.

The agonized scream shattering the night was enough to chill even raw passion.

John moved to the hut's entrance. The guard was looking towards the center of the village.

Impulse, instinct, moved him.

Without thinking, John reached for the native guard. His arm went around the man's neck, fast, squeezed tight, cutting off any sound the man might make. It happened so quickly that the stunned native had only time for a short, minor struggle. He slumped against John's body, merely writhing against the strong choking arm that was cutting the life breath out of him. John dragged the man into the hut, keeping the pressure on his throat.

Rita was cowering against the back wall, horrified at what was happening.

The man relaxed in death. John made up his mind as to what they would do next.

His short view of the center of the village had revealed enough to make him realize that their chances of escape were fairly good. It was good for his peace of mind that he hadn't seen what had the full attention of the native tribe.

He grabbed at Rita and they slipped out of the hut.

John had decided that he would search the immediate huts for Carol. If he didn't find her quickly, then he would have to leave with Rita. It was better that at least the two of them got away.

It took only a moment to spot the hut where Carol might be. A native guard was sitting by the entrance, looking toward the center of the village. John's fingers gripped the knife, which he'd taken from the native he'd killed a few moments before. Silently and quickly he crept up on the native. It took only a moment to plunge the blade into the man's throat. Without a sound the native slumped to the ground, dead.

Rita entered the hut and discovered Carol there,

still unconscious. She called to John who came into the hut, took in the situation quickly and then bent over and pulled Carol into his arms. Without a word they slipped out of the hut and started toward the edge of the village.

JUNGLE GODDESS, BY CHARLES NUETZEL

CHAPTER 9

Tortured at the Stake

The native chief had quickly pulled the knife away from Bob's throat laughingly ran its point lightly across the white man's chest, cutting a thin red line.

Bob's scream broke off at the first sensation of the stinging point cutting along his flesh.

His terror cooled; snapped off like the breaking of a twig. His vision cleared and he coolly surveyed his captors. Then he saw something that startled and overjoyed him.

Rita and John Barton were creeping toward Carol's hut. He saw the white hunter kill the guard, then watched as Rita and John disappeared into the hut.

Bob screamed again to keep the attention of the natives surrounding him.

He screamed when Barton and Rita left the hut with Carol and headed toward the jungle.

He saw Rita turn. Her eyes spotted him and she hesitated, said something to Barton. The two froze, just at the edge of the jungle, looking at him.

Go away, go away! Bob pleaded silently. Then he screamed, knowing that the natives would not understand his words: *"Leave me...for God's sake...for Carol's sake—leave me!"*

They hesitated for a moment longer and then Bob felt a thrill of relief as they quickly moved into the jungle.

The native chief stepped closer to Bob and ran his knife point once more across his chest, in the opposite direction of the first cut, making a large cross of red on the white flesh.

Bob felt a tremble of pain needle through him. Terror started to choke his throat and he fought to keep it down. *What would the Bob Lake in fiction do?* It was the only thing he could focus on. Play it out like you're writing this scene. Play that altered self!

He realized that the best chance that the other three had of making good their escape was if he put on the best damn show the natives had ever seen. With that thought, Bob let out an ear-piercing scream that sounded through the jungle like an explosion. A thrill raced through him; for the first time in his life the old Bob, the cowardly self, was able to fully surface in all its glory for a great and grand purpose. In the instant, he realized such a wave of pleasure that it overwhelmed every other reality. He screamed, almost happily, inviting the full attention of his tormenters. He screamed in thrilling pleasure that his death would serve a good, grand purpose. The cowardly Bob Lake would die in the glorious knowledge that this had given the other three whites a chance at escape and survival. What better gift than to offer one's life for that of his friends?

94

Even as he had screamed, his eyes were coldly looking at the native's face. A part of him was calculatingly aware of everything happening, even while that inner core was raging with energy so overwhelming that it was difficult to contain it.

Words formed as he looked into the native's eyes. For a moment calm teased along his mind as he said: "Go screw yourself! You son of a bitch!"

Even though the man couldn't understand the words, it was obvious that their meaning was blatantly naked in Bob's tone of voice.

Go to hell!

He focused on that thought as he once again gave in to the fury and outrage—the screams radiated out from his lungs and filled the air with their cleansing release. The self-contempt of a lifetime surfaced and vomited itself out into the night air.

The knife teased like a razor, bringing pain and blood.

At that instant reality stripped him of all sanity and he screamed in real terror of death that was certain to follow some terrible long lasting torture. He knew, instinctively, that in the next moments he'd be begging for the relief of death, and was already pleading for it to be quick.

His lips parted and his lungs released themselves of all air in a moment of utter mad terror. There was an insane relief in letting it all happen, without resistance, as if some dam had burst and all the power and force of the restraining waters power housed past the crumbling ruins of a lifetime in cowardly hell.

That scream followed by another when a spear point touched his stomach, drawing blood. Another

95

spear point cut into his flesh, followed by another and another.

Finally the screams became literal unending pleas for death.

* * * * * * *

Tallie had been in a tree, which overhung the edge of the village, and had seen what had happened below. Her sharp eyes had taken in much; her keen sense of native intelligence, told her much.

She watched Bob Lake being strapped to the pole, listened to his first scream with contempt, and then settled back to watch the show that she knew would follow.

Tallie was not basically cruel, but having lived in the jungle for so long, she had gained a mental outlook toward the world around her that made it possible to accept death and pain as a natural course of life. She admired courage and she hated cowardliness. But savage, primitive as she was, her brain was highly developed and knife sharp. She saw John Barton and Rita leave one hut; watched as the white hunter killed the second guard; saw him carrying Carol Hill out of the hut and into the jungle. She was also aware of what was happening to Bob, and his cool silence, which puzzled her. She noticed that he had seen the other three whites, and was aware of the exchange of glances. The fact that Bob started screaming again was blatantly revealing.

Tallie knew that the natives had ways of communicating ideas to one another, but she also knew what a scream meant. What was more, she knew that the first scream of terror was different from the later ones. She puzzled over this for some time, while Bob's screams became more and more like the first one.

A wounded animal screams in pain and anger. And she thought about the man's screams, and she thought about the man, too, and the strange feeling she had felt when leading him and the blonde-haired girl back to their campsite. And she remembered the thoughts that had run through her mind, earlier, when watching two monkeys mating.

All this time she was watching Bob Lake, watching as the natives, one at a time, slid their spear points into Bob's white flesh, drawing lines over his chest, until there was more red than white.

She couldn't help admiring the tense hard muscles that strained against the bonds that held the man against the stake. Many things blended together in her mind to change her attitude toward Bob. She realized that he had screamed that second time, after seeing his friends trying to reach the jungle, in order to keep the attention of the blacks. That would be obvious to anybody who saw the whole scene. The natives, though, were oblivious of the escape silently taking place behind their backs.

But what was more important, Tallie didn't like the odds against Bob. He wasn't given a fair chance to fight. Why that should matter to her was not even considered. Tallie was used to reacting instinctively; and that animal reaction to events had served to make survival possible for almost as long as she could remember. Now the vague, dreamlike strange memories of other white people like herself surfaced, once again. These whites were from that dream state of her childhood nightmares. Tallie shook that mental image off, and set her attention on what was taking place at the moment.

Tallie had never really felt a strong emotional attachment to the blacks, and had felt a certain amount of contempt at the way they hunted wild beasts, ganging up on them in packs.

She fitted an arrow to the strong bow in her hands. Under normal circumstances, a civilized man could do little to save Bob at this point, let alone a woman—a small, tiny little creature like Tallie. But the fact was that Tallie wasn't a normal woman—she hadn't been pampered by the softness of civilization. She was a savage; an agile product of the jungle. She had survived in a hellish nightmare that would have killed a normal woman years ago. She could move like lightning through the trees. She could fairly swing from branch to branch. Her reflexes were swift as electrical pulses.

Pulling back the bowstring until the arrow point was touching her right hand, Tallie aimed at the native stepping up to Bob with his spear point.

She released the bowstring and the arrow shot like lightning, toward the native, plunging deep into his back. Scarcely had he hit the ground before a second arrow was imbedded into the chest of another black, and a third winged its way toward the Chief.

The natives screamed in one voice of surprise, turning in the direction from which the arrows had come. They rushed forward, forgetting about their captive who was all but unconscious.

No sooner were they half way toward the tree in which Tallie had been, than three arrows plunged into the backs of three warriors, from the far left side of the village clearing.

It took a moment before they could adjust to this new attack. They turned, only to find more arrows on their way from another direction.

The natives were, as all savages, superstitious, and they knew of the jungle white goddess who lived in their part of the jungle, but it didn't occur to them that this attack could be coming from this one little white girl. Not until Tallie suddenly appeared at the edge of the jungle, at the far side of the village from Bob Lake, did they identify their attacker.

Anger and hate welled up through the blacks. As one body, they rushed the white girl who had dared to make an attack on their village.

Tallie waited until she was sure they were mad enough to follow her, then shooting one of the three remaining arrows in her quiver, she turned and rushed down the jungle game trails fast as her legs would carry her. She ran for a long time, the natives in hot pursuit, until she was well away from the village, and then she swung up into the trees and disappeared from sight. The natives shot past her, continuing on in what they were sure was her trail.

A thin grin spread across Tallie's lips and she quickly swung off in the direction of the village. In moments, a lot shorter time than it had taken to go by foot, Tallie reached her destination.

* * * * * * *

The moment John and Rita had entered the jungle, they started off in a fast trot. John was slowed down only slightly by the weight of the unconscious Carol. He didn't dare take the time to attempt to revive her until they were well away from the village. There was no telling when their escape would be discovered.

They hadn't gone far before Carol moaned and showed signs of reviving. She opened her eyes and for a moment didn't seem to understand where she was.

Finally Carol asked: "What's happening?"

"How do you feel?" John managed.

She shook her head, frowned and then quickly seemed to take in what was their surroundings.

John was thankful that she didn't have time to ask any questions. She indicated that she was able to make her own way and he quickly put her down on the ground. And they continued their run.

How long they continued John had no way of knowing for sure. When his lungs were about to burst from tiredness, he knew that the women were at the limit of their endurance. There was nothing else to do but stop, rest. During the last minutes they had been staggering through the jungle game trail.

The minute he indicated a stop, the two women fell to the ground, exhausted. It was some time before any of them spoke. Carol broke the silence.

"Where's Bob?" she asked in a shaky, gasping voice.

It was the first time that John allowed himself to think of the other man. Having to leave him behind had been difficult—but unavoidable. It was obvious that they could not have saved the man.

"What happened?" Carol demanded, alarm flaring in her eyes.

"There wasn't anything we could do...to

save…Bob," John finally said in a low, sick voice.

Carol stared at him for a long time and then tears slowly welled in her eyes.

Neither John nor Rita moved. Each was trapped in their own depth of agony at what had happened.

Their situation was, at best, hopeless. Without weapons, supplies, blankets, their chance of reaching civilization was almost nil. Bob's fate, in a way, to John, seemed almost kind under the circumstances. At least he would be dead by the evening—while they would have to fight their way through the jungle, dying one at a time, always on edge of hope that somehow they would make it back to civilization. And moment by moment proving the mockery of that hope; a quick death would certainly end the suspense—and useless struggle for survival. That thought clawed at the back of his mind for but a moment, then John forced himself to face the fact that no matter how small their chances were, at least they had a slim one. Bob Lake didn't even have that! Hopefully he was dead by now; but John guessed otherwise. The torture would be long lasting—death would come after hours of pain had driven sanity away.

Determined not to share his thoughts with the women, he merely shrugged them off and slowly stood.

"We better get moving," he announced.

The two women hesitated for a moment and then Rita turned towards him, face contorted, body trembling.

"What the *hell* can *we* do?" she screamed. "We'll *never* make it!"

John moved fast, knowing what was coming,

101

knowing the only way to stop it.

"We're alive! That's something! While we live there's always a chance."

Rita just stood there, staring, saying nothing.

John turned to Carol, expecting an outburst from her, too, but she squared her shoulders.

"Let's start," she suggested in a brave but shaking voice.

"Come," John Barton said. "We can't stay long in any one place...we have to get as much space between us and those savages as possible."

As they started off, John felt depression hit him once again, digging deep like clawing fingers at his inner core. What chance did they really have? How could they possibly make it through the long miles—how many he didn't even know for sure—which stretched out between them and any outpost of civilization? And what lay between them and safety? What other savages would they have to face? It seemed completely hopeless, but the human animal is such that even in the face of hopelessness, it will fight to the bitter end to hold on to life

They were walking along a game trail, through which countless animals had trampled a pathway, and suddenly they came to a turn and found themselves at the bank of a river.

Hope touched John Barton. The river had to lead to the ocean, and to civilization. But the river also meant native settlements and danger. He was on the point of attempting to decide the best plan that would give them the most safety when suddenly from behind came the low threatening growl of a lion.

They turned as one body and found themselves

facing a large magnificent lion who was snarling threateningly at them.

JUNGLE GODDESS, BY CHARLES NUETZEL

CHAPTER 10

Tallie Unleashed

For Bob Lake the blanket of terrifying pain had suddenly shattered; it was like awakening from a consuming nightmare. Slowly he was aware of one simple fact. They had stopped torturing him. Why, he didn't know. There wasn't enough strength in his body to attempt to think or reason out an answer. It was obvious that to this point the torture had been minor.

He stood there, slumped against the post to which he was tied, thanking God for this one last moment of respite. And wondering what to expect next. The final thrust of a blade into his heart, bringing a final, embracing end to all this hell?

A terrible part of him accepted the fact that death was at best moments away—and actually probably after hours of horrifying pain. In either case he was doomed. And in that conviction came another sense of truth: if he were to survive this nothing would scare him again—a rebirth would surely being a new Bob Lake. All the fantasy terrors of a lifetime could not match this harsh reality—and nothing life might offer could ever be this terrible. But it was too late...he would die soon enough—in fact not soon enough!

How long the torture would last he didn't know. His mind was dazed and numbed; it could have been a moment and it could have been an hour, he didn't know. Suddenly he felt delicate fingers touching his hands that were so tightly bound behind him, around the post.

He felt a sudden movement and a sudden release. Bob slumped to the ground, his face eating into the dirt.

Two hands reached for him, taking an arm, attempting to drag him along the ground, a soft wordless sound spoke to him. Bob opened his eyes, turned his head.

What was happening? He didn't know at first. Then his mind snapped to attention.

The jungle girl. How had it happened?

Where were the natives?

Bob struggled to his feet.

The jungle girl was quick to motion him to follow her. The moment they were surrounded by foliage, she climbed into a tree, paused at a branch and looked down at him. Under normal circumstances, Bob would have shuddered at the implication of what her action was suggesting. Weakened and exhausted, it was impossible.

The girl stared at him for a moment and then she quickly swung down to the ground, taking hold of his hand and leading the way through the jungle.

Bob staggered after her, half stumbling, dazed from what he'd been through in the last hours. Desperation and the instinctive drive to survive gave him strength—but nothing more. His mind couldn't digest what was happening; it was only possible to react, without consideration. He followed the mysterious young woman, unconcerned at to his fate in her hands.

They had gone a little over a mile along the game trail when the jungle girl pulled him into the foliage and then led the way down to a small ravine, along which she took up their march. On and on they went and every step seemed an eternity. He kept telling himself that he had to continue, had to take that one more step, and again the next step, until they were completely safe. He didn't doubt that this savage girl had a destination in mind, a place where they would be safe from the bastards who had tried to kill him.

A couple of times they passed animals, but Bob only vaguely noticed. He kept his eyes on the naked girl in front of him. When exhaustion had taken what little strength seemed left to him, Bob forced his attention to the girl's dainty body, the golden glow of her flesh. The lightheaded fever that washed over him might have been caused by those erotic images, but most likely had more to do with a physical reaction to what had happened to him. It was like being drawn into a deep dark well, drowning in flames. His thoughts became blurry, the world slightly out of focus. Bob forced himself to concentrate on the beauty of the little jungle nymph in front of him. Fevered nor not; that was the most enjoyable fantasy his mind could embrace. He attempted to imagine what it must be like to embrace her. In one of his "adventure books" anything might take place—whatever his imagination could create. He forced himself to think in terms of sensual intimacy in a desperate effort to escape from the agony of just taking another step; like a man attempting to hypnotize himself into doing the impossible he found himself wondering what she might want with him; what she might do to him; what kind of savage mate.... The images shivered like a fevered dream, faded and then reshaped, tangling together with the reality still clawing at his body. Every step was a hell. He tried to imagine what kind of pleasure this jungle creature might offer in some distant future just beyond his reach. The visions shattered again and reality crushed back into being.

As the jungle girl turned away from the small ravine, Bob stumbled, fell to the ground, his face splashing into the shallow water. He couldn't move another inch, his muscles tensed in one last attempt to move; his mind tried to recapture the erotic vision of being held close to the girl's naked body, but even that was far too difficult to do. Bob Lake's mind and body just shuttered and then relaxed in unconsciousness.

* * * * * * *

The natives had been running through the jungle, along the game trail for a long time, the leading ones began to doubt the possibility of finding the jungle girl, whom they called Tallie. They came to a sudden turn and then found themselves facing a lion and the three whites they had believed were still held captive in their village.

With a roar of rage, they charged, forgetting the lion that froze but for a moment and then turned, facing this new more deadly threat.

Carol saw the lion first, then the natives. All

hope rushed out of her. For a moment she almost fell to the ground in a dead faint. Only by strong will power was she able to remain standing.

John Barton had stepped between her and Rita the moment he saw the lion, apparently in the hope of at least giving the girls a chance at some how getting away.

Then the lion turned and growled at the natives, who suddenly came to a startled halt.

Barton moved fast. "Back up—slowly, into the river—don't panic!"

The lion's tail slowly swung from left to right and then snapped straight out as its muscles tensed for a leap.

The natives swung their spears high over their heads and then threw them with all the strength of their bodies toward the lion. A couple made their mark as the beast leaped forward into a death charge.

A couple of spears flew past the lion, just missing them. John moved fast, picking up the weapons and then motioned the women into the river.

"Fast...we might have a...chance..."

Carol felt the chilly waters circle around her feet and legs. Then suddenly the bottom dropped out from under her and she started swimming desperately. Barton shouted directions at them and they started heading down river, toward the other bank some fifty yards away. The man fell behind the women in his attempt to keep hold of the two spears.

Carol was first to reach the shore on the other side of the river. She turned and waited until Rita came to her side, and helped the other woman up to the dry land.

They watched as Barton swam toward them. He had a little over ten yards to go when Carol spotted an ugly reptile head skimming the water a short ten feet away from the hunter.

"John!" she shouted, "behind you!"

Barton didn't even turn, but seemed to redouble his efforts to make it to the shore in time. In the process he lost one of the spears, but that made it easier to span the rest of the distance.

The crocodile shot quickly after the man, determined not to lose its afternoon meal. It was too close a chase for Carol to watch, but she couldn't keep her eyes off the drama taking place.

With Barton alive they had little chance of getting beyond the next day alive—without him, they had *no* chance at all.

It seemed an eternity, as if time stood still, as if every stroke the man made through the water were taking an hour to make.

They watched, horrified, as the crocodile slowly closed the distance between itself and John Barton.

Then, finally, the man reached the shore, threw the spear toward Carol, and pulled himself up out of the water just as the crocodile was within reach.

As he stood, the reptile lunged out after him.

Carol swooped up the spear and stepped bravely forward. But what could she do against such a terrible creature with only a spear in her hand? As the crocodile opened its huge mouth, revealing a double row of jagged, deadly teeth, Carol rammed the spear into that gapping cavity and leaped away. The reptile slammed its mouth down on the wooden shaft, which snapped in two under the powerful vice of those horrible jaws.

None of the trio watched to see what happened after that; they turned and fled into the jungle, attempting to get as much distance between themselves and the river. They hadn't gone far before the earth suddenly slipped out from under them, and like three trees being sucked into the earth during an earthquake, they tumbled down into the dark cavity that had opened up under them.

* * * * * * *

Tallie knew that she had to get the white man on his feet again. It could be only a matter of time before the natives discovered his disappearance and they would be in a holy rage; angrier than the gods when they did battle in the skies.

She bent over the still form of Bob Lake and then turned him over. After examining his wounds, she discovered they were minor, though she washed them in the water. The man moaned, but remained unconscious until she splashed water over his face. His eyes fluttered, but nothing more. Tallie then shook him much like a jungle cat would shake its kill.

A soft moan sounded from his lips and then slowly his eyes fluttered open. For a moment the man lay there as if dazed and unable to remember where he was. Then he saw the features of Tallie leaning over him and a crooked smile played on his mouth.

Tallie felt an excited flutter rush through her. Now they could start again.

She pulled on the man's arm and shoulder, attempting to raise him to his feet. He hesitated and then groaned. After a moment he stood and followed Tallie

111

through the underbrush.

They continued for a long time and Tallie kept thinking about the man following her. The thoughts were strange and new to her. The feel of the man, every time she touched him, was strangely enjoyable in an oddly overwhelming way. She found it all somewhat annoying.

Finally they came to the small cliff side that broke out of the jungle. Here they could climb to a comfortable cave she visited from time to time.

There was a narrow ledge that cut up the side of the cliff and up this Tallie led the man.

The moment they were inside, Bob fell exhausted to the cave floor. Tallie watched him while he lay there, breathing hard, until the rising and falling of his chest had calmed and she was assured he was asleep.

She examined the spear wounds in his chest and then left the cave to get some water and leaves that she knew had healing qualities that would soothe the cuts which had been inflicted on the man. They didn't seem serious—just painful.

While she was gone from the cave, Bob stirred and rolled over. He was dreaming about Tallie. Then he felt hands moving over his chest and the thoughts faded away.

Tallie cleaned the wounds and then lay the broad leaves over them, holding them down against the open cuts. She sat there for a long, long time, watching the man, enjoying the action of touching him. She ran her fingers along the hard muscles of his shoulders and arms, over his face.

He was a good-looking god, she thought, well

pleased.

She remembered the monkeys and the jungle animals, and most of all the mating of the village natives. She thought about such things and looked at the man lying asleep next to her and wondered if he might become her mate. They were the innocent thoughts of a virginal being that had never known anything other than the jungle life around her. She knew what took place between the wild beasts and the black men of the forest. Vague ancient memories—images that haunted her dreams—momentarily flashed in her mind of tall gods and goddess' embracing, murmuring strange sounds that almost seem understandable. All these internal visions had puzzled her for as long as she could remember. They were vague and strange. Yet somehow seemed like memories rather than nightmares. They blended with the visions of natives mating in the bushes, monkeys, and beasts dancing out their courtships to final unions. She vaguely understood such things, but had never had a mate of her own.

These thoughts teased her and she smiled silently while looking at this white man sleeping there near her.

Yes, she decided, *she would have him as a mate.*

It was as simple as that to Tallie. She knew that the jungle animals seemed to enjoy themselves in such casual, delightful acts and she knew that the natives seemed to highly enjoy mating; and most of all she enjoyed touching the man lying next to her—she enjoyed that very, very much.

Some lonely spark that had never been alive was beginning to flame within Tallie. Like all creatures of the world, she was no different in wanting the companionship of those of her own kind. Now, having been exposed, just this short time, to a male, she knew it to be good and nice and wanted it to never stop. A very strange thought, a very odd desire that nonetheless seemed quite natural. Tallie didn't question her feelings; just simply enjoyed them. She could do nothing else but delight in its seductive offerings. She mused them into a mental reality of what might happen, then smiled again.

Life was a simple experience of moving from one living act to another—accepting whatever happened. Joy, pain, hunger, tiredness; all were a part of her everyday existence.

The last thought in her mind, before sleep gently took consciousness away, was that she had a mate of her own, like all the others in her jungle world, and she was happy and content. It was that simple.

CHAPTER 11

The Jungle Goddess

Barton was first to realize what had happened. The moment he hit the bottom of the pit he sprang to his feet, taking in the earthen walls that surrounded them.

Rita screamed out hysterically, Carol lay still, where she had fallen.

"Quiet!" John Barton demanded. "We're lucky this wasn't staked." The very thought of the strong stakes, pointing upwards to impale anything that fell into the hunting pit, shot a shudder through John. After a quick examination, he discovered that it would be an easy matter to climb out, back on solid ground again.

"Here, Rita...I'll give you a hand."

The woman had been quiet from the first word John had spoken and now she stepped up to him, hugging close. "I'm scared. I know we won't get out of this alive. I know I'm going to die—and I don't want to die—oh, John...John!"

She hugged to him, shaking.

John put a protective arm around her shoulder

and felt a wave of tenderness ebbing through him. It was impossible not to be responsive. Spoiled, selfish rich girl—lost little child; lustful woman—it didn't matter! His natural instinct had built-in responses; and the woman was far from unattractive!

But this was hardly the time for such interludes.

And this wasn't the time to entertain mental investigations into what drove Rita. Best to simply be aware she was unstable. What had happened in the hut between them had to be forgotten—it wasn't something he felt good about. Regardless.

He gently held her. "As long as we're alive, Rita, there's a chance. We can't keep thinking about anything else. Keep telling yourself that everything will be all right! Believe that and you'll have the strength to continue. You have to believe it!"

He looked down into her eyes and saw a sudden, slow change take place. It was as if she were gaining strength from him. Her jaw tightened and then she smiled.

"Thank God for you, John. Help me up! Up there!" Her voice was sharp and level as she glanced at the edge of the pit above them.

Barton lifted Rita up until it was possible for her to climb the rest of the way.

John turned to Carol. From outward appearances she was no more than badly bruised, but unconscious. Though her shirt had been ripped open slightly, almost torn from her body.

As he started to lift her, Carol's eyes fluttered and then opened.

"You're all right," John quickly told her. "We fell into a bloody pit some native tribe had dug for

116

animals. Think you can stand?"

She slowly came to her feet and then brushed herself off, as if it were important to keep her clothing clean. Then for the first time she seemed to realize her semi-nakedness.

A red blush colored her cheeks as she turned away, presenting her back to him.

She is a lovely woman, John thought, having actually noticed her full youthful breasts for the first time. How wonderful she looked. A very real surge of desire ebbed up through him; he tried to ignore it, but didn't want to. Carol sparked a core deep inside him which was far different from mere lust—yet that was there fully realized, too, by the vision of her standing there before him.

"Here," he said, starting to unbutton his shirt "You can wear this...it's a bit large...but it'll be better than nothing."

Carol seemed to hesitate and then shrugged her shoulders. She turned and faced him, unembarrassed.

"I guess this is a hell of a time to be modest," she laughed.

Rita's voice called down to them. It was sharp and nasty sounding. "What's going on down there?"

She hadn't missed a beat and her eyes revealed she knew exactly what was going on.

John looked up and saw Rita's face, which was hardened with raw, hateful jealousy. He almost laughed, because there wasn't really anything for Rita to be jealous about. He had no designs on either of them. He had no plans for anything other than survival.

Only madness would suggest otherwise.

Carol pulled on his tan shirt and then buttoned it over her breasts. Then John Barton lifted her up in his arms, then higher, holding her by the waist until she could reach the top of the pit and pull herself the rest of the way with Rita's reluctant help.

Once Carol was standing beside Rita, John stepped back to the other side of the pit and made a short running leap. The first time he missed the top by only inches. The second attempt his fingers gripped hold of the edge and he dug his feet into the wall of earth next to his body. Straining every muscle, John pulled himself upwards until he was finally able to drag his body over the edge.

Standing, he looked at the two women, and for the first time realized the full extent of their situation. Under the right circumstances, on an isolated island, with these two women, it would hardly be an undesirable exile!

"Let's get started again," he suggested, stepping past the women and moving to a tree, and reaching for a small branch that looked easy enough to break off. Once he had broken it off, he trimmed the foliage off and then turned, looked at the women.

"This time...we take it easier. We'll find a camp site and then I'll see about making some weapons...a spear might come in handy, now and then," he pointed out. Taking the stick he moved in front of the two women and then poked the ground in front of him. Every step he took was carefully controlled, testing. He didn't want to take the chance of running into another animal trap—this time possibly staked.

They continued on for several hours until they came to a clearing next to a small brook. It was getting late and the sun was beginning to set on the western horizon behind them.

John Barton chose this as a logical campsite. "You girls can take a bath, if you want...and I'll start gathering wood for a fire and..."

"Let me," Carol offered, "get the wood. You can look for something to make a...spear with."

Rita was quick to follow Carol's suggestion and the three went about the business of organizing camp. They had gathered some fruits and berries along the way, and now devoured them hungrily.

It was getting dark by the time Barton had a fire going. He sat by the small flames and started stripping the strong, thick shaft he had managed to get from one of the trees surrounding the camp.

Carol had disappeared around a corner of the brush and undressed and was splashing in the small brook which just covered her body when she lay down in the water.

Rita came up to John, stood over him. She knelt beside him, touching his bare shoulder.

"What's with you and Carol?" Rita inquired, almost innocently.

"What're you talking about?"

"Oh, come on, I saw the way you all but fairly feasted on her naked breasts back in that pit! Your eyes—"

"Stop right there!" he warned, stiffening. "This isn't the time or the place—"

"Oh, I don't know about that," Rita murmured quite seductively. "What's left outside of death? I'd rather die in ecstasy! If we don't survive...what does it matter?"

119

She laughed at that, a bit hysterically. "I'll admit it. I'm basic. Money is a powerful seducer! And what Rita wants…she gets in the end."

"Yes," he admitted, "I suppose so, from most people. But money won't get you out of this situation!"

"You mean: *crappy* situation!" Her words were bitter. Then her mood changed, becoming almost frightened. "Quite frankly, I *am* scared."

He glanced at her, but the expression in her eyes was unnervingly brazen as they swept over his half naked body.

She smiled, lips half parted.

When he didn't say anything, returning his attention to stripping the shaft free of foliage, Rita gripped hold of his arm, tensing her fingers on the hard steel of his muscle. "You're strong, John. I like strong—I'm not that strong. I liked what happened…back there…between us! I'm frightened. I'm scared. I need your strength! In the way a woman need's a—"

"Stop it, Rita! Wrong time, wrong place! And you know it!" he snapped, jerking his arm away from her grip.

He refused to look at her.

"Why, because of Carol? I don't think she would mind. Now why should she?"

He looked stonily into her eyes. "Knock it off, Rita!"

She winced as if slapped. Her whole frame went rigid and her eyes narrowed into slits. "Don't you *dare* tell me…how dare you!"

"Stop!" he warned as she started to move towards him. "Just stop playing games!"

She frowned, then, again, the mood changed like the flipping of a coin: "I'm not playing games, dearie. Most people in this setting would screw their heads off!"

She laughed throatily. "Well, people like me! Now don't tell me you aren't aware of that! In your line of business! A handsome man like you, John. Surely a lot of ladies have demanded your...well... special talents! I'm sure they expect the Big White Hunter, Big Bwana, to offer up those extra good-ies...that they *paid* for as *part of the deal!* And I kept that...polite, if you noticed!" She laughed shrilly. "Now, ain't I nice?"

"Cut it."

She laughed at that, then added, almost in a stage whisper: "Come on, you deliciously big jungle beast!"

She moved very close to him, suddenly, her hips slightly thrust forward. Her lips were upturned towards his.

With another woman it might be different; or even with Rita under different circumstances. But here, and now it was a joke! No way.

"Don't you want it?" she demanded, a sharp edge to her voice. She opened the top button of her shirt, then the second, almost exposing her breasts. He reached out and grabbed her hand before she could loosen another button. "Oh, how strong you are, John! You were *so* good! And you *do* want me, don't you?" She literally pressed herself against his hand. Her breast was warm, so soft, full and firm. "I need it, John, oh *how* I need it! You can't imagine how *bad* I

121

need it." Her voice was thick with hungry desperation.

He attempted to back away, but she surged forward, against him, murmured softly: "And what Rita wants, Rita gets!"

That last was a seductive mantra.

She suddenly threw her arms around him. Her body caressed his. He could feel a naked breast against his chest. For only a moment it was almost impossible to resist.

Very firmly, yet gently, he took her wrists and moved her back. "No!"

Rita snapped: "How *dare* you!"

Her face contorted in rage. For several moments she glared at him. Then she glanced over his shoulder, towards where Carol Hill had disappeared.

"It's all *her* fault. You want *that* bitch! Of *course*! That's *it*!" she fairly screamed.

He merely glared at her, not moving.

"It *is* Carol, isn't it? She's had her eye on you all along. The little whore! And *you* want *her*!"

He wanted to hit her, hard.

"You'd screw her bloody ass off if she's offer it to you!" Rita fairly screamed at him, now quite hysterical.

"What's wrong with you?" was all he could think of saying. Denying any interest in Carol would solve nothing. And he realized that Rita was right.

"But you *won't* have her. John, you simply *won't*." The woman suddenly arched forward, threateningly, eyes wide with fury. "I'd kill her first—simply that."

"Christ, Rita, what are you talking about?"

"I'd kill the bitch!" she almost hissed between

clinched teeth. The woman's eyes were wide, glassy as they met his.

"I'll kill the whoring bitch!" she muttered.

Then without any warning at all Rita leaped away, turning, running for the brook in which Carol was swimming.

John rushed after her, realizing from the almost insane look in the woman's eyes that she was quite able to follow through with her threat.

* * * * * * *

At about that same time, Bob suddenly awoke to find himself lying next to the jungle nymph who had saved his life. What followed was experienced through a mental daze, as if created by some fevered dream. He sat up, hardly realizing where he was. The wounds were only dim background, numbed. His whole focus was on the woman.

Tallie jerked up, springing to her feet. Her eyes searched the cave and entrance as if expecting attack. Then she looked at him and a slow happy smile broke across her lush lips.

She pointed to herself, said: "Tallie!"

Bob laughed and then pointed to himself: "Bob!"

"Boob?" she echoed.

"Bob!"

"Bob." Then tapping her naked chest, "Tallie."

"Tallie—that's a nice name. Where do you come from?"

She shook her head, then suddenly came closer, standing only inches from him. A strange, questioning

123

expression clouded her features. Her body touched his, eyes puzzled. She stood there as if expecting something to happen.

Bob had lots of thoughts about what could happen if she continued to stand there, naked and sexy as all hell. In a book it might be a natural setup for a seduction scene. In reality it was much more than that; a terribly teasing temptation; all but overwhelming.

Gently he took hold of her shoulders and urged her away from him, shaking his head from side to side to indicate she wasn't to do that again.

She frowned and the moment he released her shoulders stepped forward, this time much closer. He could feel the brush of her nipples tease his flesh.

"No, Tallie!" he said in a firm voice, pushing her away, fighting an automatic urge to ravish the hell out of her.

Bob didn't miss the implications. Who would know the difference? Nothing "civilized" needed to apply. Only the moment counted. Nothing more. And in one of his books it might have happened quite naturally. The primitive young women would overwhelm the hero and they'd fall passionately into one another's arms. Regardless of how unrealistic that might be. Nobody could blame him for taking her obvious offer.

He studied the woman and toyed with his imagined fantasy....

If she wanted it, he could have her.

He urged her away, back, at arms length. "No!"

The minute he released her, Tallie stepped closer again, this time circling his chest with her arms, holding tight, with all her strength.

The nearness, the soft texture of her tanned skin

124

against his chest created a hot fiery reaction in Bob. It was impossible to ignore it. Even against the numbed burn of the stinging cuts that the native spear points had inflicted on his chest, he felt a wild, almost uncontrollable excitement surge through him. How easy to give in at this moment; to fold her into his arms and fairly devour the innocent offering, the delicious wonder of her young body. The mere idea was like a drug to him.

"Tallie! No!"

It must have been something in his voice that finally got to Tallie. She slowly relaxed and then bounced away. She studied Bob for a long time and then her face brightened and she lay down on the floor of the cave and reached up arms in simple offering.

He turned away, trying to ignore the blunt suggestive way she was presenting herself. Was it natural instinct? She appeared like a woman openly offering herself to a lover, without strings, without thought of anything other than their mutual union.

Bob realized he was probably in a state of shock from all that had happened. The torture had driven him illusionary. Certainly the sight of this female didn't do much to sooth that madness.

"Bob—Bob—Bob—" Tallie chanted over and over again, laughing, giggling, hauntingly calling to him to come to her.

Bob moved to the front of the cave and looked out over the jungle. He felt drunk. Or drugged.

He wanted to ignore the jungle girl's chanting. He tried to think about Rita and Carol and John Barton. They were, if still alive, somewhere out there in the jungle convinced that he was already dead. He was as good as dead. The thought drove deep searing pain through him.

How was he ever to get out of this hellish jungle? There couldn't be many hours left before life was squashed out of existence. He didn't want to face that! Escape of any kind was all he wanted. No booze. Just this lovely young girl.

Nothing seemed real, any more. Morality be damned!

He turned away from the jungle and his eyes fell on the reposed form of Tallie.

What an inviting sight. How primitive and natural. She had saved his life; he would be dead by now except for her.

"Bob. Bob. Bob," she kept chanting. Maybe all she wanted was closeness.

That's it, he rationalized in his fevered desperation to find reasoned excuse for what was sure to follow.

Her arms reached out like a little child's, her eyes pleaded with his. He felt dizzy and as if caught in some haunting dream—this couldn't really be happening. It was an illusion of a mind gone mad. He was dying somewhere; back there—maybe dying at the stake where the natives were continuing to probe his body with naked spear points.

That made more sense that this vision lying on the cave floor.

"Could you possibly know what you're doing?" he asked.

Her face brightened happily at his words, as if they were some secret love sounds. It was a natural action of joy and excitement.

126

Yet, her actions were those of a woman who is doing something she had seen done—but never personally acted out.

Bob sat down, shook his head, tried to keep his eyes away from her.

Finally, Tallie stood, came over to him, leaned as close as she could get, attempting to be as near as possible. Her delicate fingers caressed lightly over the muscles of his arm and shoulder. The touch was electric and so damned pleasant that it was impossible to ignore them. He wanted to stop her. He wanted to make her understand that she shouldn't do such things.

But he wanted her more!

As he turned to gently push her away, Bob found himself staring into pleading, wide blue innocent eyes. Her lips, soft, naturally deep red, so close, so tempting, so impossible to resist. And the madness overwhelmed reality and without wanting to he found himself drawn into that illusion—not even sure if it was real, convinced he was having a last erotic fantasy before death took him.

In reality he must still be tied to that stake, being tortured to death.

He decided this was all the illusion of a dying mind.

Bob Lake embraced the fantasy with his total being. If he must die, then let it be in the arms of this fantasy creature, clutched in the pleasure of imagined ecstasy as death claimed him.

JUNGLE GODDESS, BY CHARLES NUETZEL

CHAPTER 12

Jungle Passions

Carol was enjoying herself, lounging in the water, dreaming of the safety and security of the United States—which she might never see again. Oddly enough the harsh reality of their situation had brought a sense of cold acceptance. All they could do was attempt to survive; if that didn't happen, then it was wise to make the best of what time they had. And so she had decided to enjoy her bath in the middle of the jungle.

She heard Rita's and John's loud voices shouting at each other. Then the sound of rushing feet coming toward her.

Startled, Carol tried to hide herself under the shallow water, not considering that there was any threat of violence coming toward her; only automatically attempting to cover her nakedness in case John Barton were to come on the scene.

Rita leaped out of the clearing, down toward her, face contorted like an escapee from an insane ward.

129

It was Carol's first warning of impending danger.

There was something about the look on the other woman's face that checked Carol's modesty and shot sudden fear through her.

Rita came right toward her, not breaking pace.

The woman merely screamed.

Carol couldn't possibly guess what had happened, or what could have caused Rita to charge her. In fact, at first, Carol couldn't really accept the fact that the other woman was actually about to attack her. She was on the point of convincing herself that Rita was merely running from some unknown or imagined threat, when the woman drove right at her, murderous rage in her eyes.

Startled, hardly prepared for what was happening, Carol attempted to ward off the other woman.

Rita's hands reached out and found Carol's throat, her face driving against Carol's head, pushing it down into the water.

Carol felt panic and shock, but also reacted in a wild attempt to save herself from this unprovoked attack. While she struggled to get her head above water, her mind was screaming in shock at what was happening.

She whipped around, gasped for air that wouldn't come. The fingers, strong with insane rage, were squeezing the life out of her. Carol suddenly realized that she had to do something fast. With all her strength she lifted up from the bottom of the brook, twisted, pulling on Rita's long black hair with all the power in her hand. It was a struggle in silence which seemed to last forever. The air was bursting in her lungs; she felt blackness ebb over her vision.

Then Carol kicked upwards into Rita's groin and the woman released the iron grip on her neck. Carol pulled away from the enraged female.

At that point John Barton leaped between them, dragged Rita to a standing position and then smashed his fist powerfully against the woman's jaw as if attempting to kill a bull elephant.

Rita stared at him for a moment as her head whipped back, and then she slumped limp in his arms.

Lifting the woman up, John carried her back to the shore.

"I'll explain later," he said.

Carol had forgotten about her nakedness and suddenly discovered she wasn't the least embarrassed. The jungle had already made a vivid change in her outlook on life. They were savages in a savage land where civilized morality and customs had no reason or point.

Gathering her clothing she followed the man into the camp. When he had roughly thrown Rita on the ground near the fire, Carol rushed up to his side and asked:

"What the hell happened?"

John turned and then his eyes stripped over her body. It was the automatic reaction of a man who finds himself in the presence of a beautiful naked woman. And, automatically, a light of interest burned bright. Then he looked away. "You better get dressed!"

"What happened?"' Carol demanded, ignoring his command, and enjoying the man's obvious discomfort.

Signing, Barton told her about Rita, making a point to keep his eyes away from her body. "Rita made a pass; I blocked it. She turned her rage on you. She had no reason...to feel that way," he stated, but the look he gave Carol brought doubt to those words. "I mean...well...you know what I mean!"

Carol felt a thrill wave through her when he finished.

"I suppose so," was all she could say at that moment.

She was surprised at what he said but also pleased. Rita was jealous of *her!* Carol couldn't help feeling flattered. And horrified.

But there was far more to what his words stated.

"I was warned about her," she offered. "Told she might be erratic, but..."

"So was I. By your publisher, to be frank."

"He believes her rep—fed by all those nasty stories," she noted, thoughtfully.

"The tabloids are crap." He sounded honestly frustrated. "One damned unstable lady! And we don't need that right now!"

"I'm sure she'll be okay."

"If not I'll have to pop her again! And believe me, I don't go around hitting women!"

"Glad you made an exception!" Carol admitted. Then more hopefully, added: "That scares me! What she did...why?"

"Under stress the best of us can go quite mad! And Miss Bentley isn't any exception!" He knelt down by the fire and picked up the shaft he had been working on before Rita had made her advances toward him. "People can also do amazingly brave acts—or cowardly ones. That woman there...well, to be blunt, is on overdrive. I've known a few like her...they want thrills and figure a Great White Hunter is Thrill Number One. Well on safari, anyway! A bit boring, to be truthful."

"Oh, really?" she laughed. "I can't believe that! A robust, healthy, normal, red-blooded male like you."

"Oh? Not you, too!" he chuckled.

"I'm just considering the facts," she countered, firmly.

He said nothing to that, but simply focused on the shaft in his hands.

Carol watched him, feeling a sudden wave of excitement.

As she looked at the tall white hunter, possibly the last white man she would ever see again, her found herself fighting a natural desire and physical need. Under the right circumstances she'd consider him a prime catch! That realization stunned Carol. Yet it would be easy to fall for the guy.

A caressing shiver raced down her spine and it was impossible to shake off the building desire. She almost welcomed it. What better way to die than in the arms of such a man! Right there in the jungle. Career, ambition, dreams, all faded under these circumstances. Suddenly the only desire left was to survive, live, make the most of what moments or days might remain to her. And in the arms of such a man it would be a wonderful experience!

The thought surprised, shocked and pleased her.

Carol drew John's shirt around her with a deep inner sense of pleasure. It was the best thing to being held in his arms.

Funny, she admitted, without embarrassment, how attitudes can change under pressure. In the civilized world she had never felt quite like this. Or would she?

We're all beasts, she realized, with some humor. *And I'm hardly a virgin*!

Carol sat down beside the man and tried to turn her thoughts to other subjects. But the lingering desire kept teasing her mind. How interesting to spend a lifetime with such a man! And, as things stood, that's exactly what she might be doing: spending the last moments of her life with John Barton!

* * * * * * *

Bob would never have expected anything like this to happen; not even in the wild "true" adventures which had made him famous. It was something out of the make-believe of reality; that zone where all things that are fantastic and impossible really happen—things that could never be put in the annals of magazine stories or books. Those fictions could not even touch the reality and beauty of what was happening.

The very naturalness of making love to this innocent little jungle nymph made it the most beautiful experience in his life.

The way she clung so child-like in his arms, murmuring, smiling up into his eyes with an emotion that she must have never felt before, cut deep at him, bringing the intense feeling to a point of desperate need. How many men had ever had the chance to teach such a woman the joys of love; this jungle girl who knew little or nothing about the real pleasures the body could rush through her?

Or had it all been a dizzy, fevered dream? He

134

really wasn't quite sure.

It was like diving into a pool of grain alcohol. He was drunk with the emotional feelings that surged over him at her nearness. Her beauty was that of nature, of perfection and simplicity. Her body firm, yet soft and yielding as only a child of nature can be; and it had overwhelmed him. She was all that God could make a woman; she had all the perfection that a man might desire in his woman.

And the feel of her flesh yielding hungrily to his thrusts, enveloping him in such passionately warm embraces, clinging to him as if never wanting to let the ecstasy end, it was all beyond imagination. He could never have captured it in words; never written his experiences down on paper. This was something beyond any dream he might have manufactured for publication.

All he knew was it would be worth dying for such an experience; to die in her arms, at the peak of their shared ecstatic rapture.

A mood, a desire, an action; total union as only a man and woman would fully experience.

But had it really taken place? He wondered. *And did it even matter?* At least they had this momentary connection, a kind of physical intimacy that came from mere nearness, touching, mere physical contact.

His mind played over what he was uncertain had actually taken place.

He had slid down along side Tallie and folded her into his arms. They lay there for several moments, just aware of the feel of one another, content to be so close.

It was so beautiful, so wonderful, such a moment of perfection that he felt the emotion choke at every muscle and nerve within him. And when he pulled her tighter to him, it seemed as if this was meant to be, as if no matter what anybody on earth might have done in an attempt to keep it from happening it would have been impossible to stop. His lips found hers, instinctively parted in open invitation. After that it was a mere matter of discovering all of her, running his kisses down along her firm, pert breasts, headily drawing the nipples between his lips, as she moaned in pleasure. After that it was the total discovery of the woman as he flowed into her again and again, unable to stop, driven by her own eager body. Tallie matched every movement, flooding around him like hot fire, drawing him deeper, more fully possessed by her young flesh. He couldn't have stopped if he'd wanted to. She was bodily locked to him, legs enveloped around him as the rest of her enveloped him, embraced him, fully surging like a pumping heart in rhythm with his own. The world of reality had shattered in this mad dreamlike passion. He was drowning in it, and nothing else existed.

How long that had lasted he didn't know. But it was there, at least in his mind, in his make-believe fantasy. The universe returned and he was lying next to her, floating above her…and simply sitting there looking down at this jungle nymph, the jungle goddess of innocence.

Bob wondered about this young woman lying there. Where had she come from? How had she gotten into the jungle? How could she have possibly survived against such impossible odds. A real mystery, which might never be untangled, but what a story she might be able to tell. What a tangled puzzle to be opened and revealed. What a book that would make! *The Jungle Goddess Mates with Bob Lake.* He literally laughed at that.

"You gotta be kidding!" he muttered. Yet quite obviously his mind was returning to normal—the writer's instinct for an instant best seller! Carol Hill had been right; but for the wrong reasons—or, at least, not enough of the real reasons! Would it ever be possible to tell the story of this jungle nymph—this goddess of nature?

He wondered, wished, hoped, and for a few pleasant moments dreamed it might be possible. They would return to civilization and somehow he'd discover her story and they would fall madly in love and be together for the rest of their lives, living off the income from the book he could write about his Jungle Goddess. Maybe even sell it to Hollywood as a major adventure film!

An instant bestseller, he told himself.

A damn good reason to survive.

Somehow!

He never knew how long he sat there dreaming, imagining a life with this lovely young creature. Would they live in a civilized world or on some island? Would she easily adapt to life in the city? Or would he have to submit to a primitive existence in a world more natural to her "living standards"? Such problems teased his writer's instinct and his natural male attraction to this lovely, innocent young creature of the jungle. These matters, surely, he reasoned, would smooth themselves out like the second draft of a novel.

Finally Tallie stirred and then sat up, smiling down at him.

"Tallie, Bob!" she laughed, tapping first herself and then his chest. "Tallie—Bob!"

It was that old movie "Me Tarzan, you Jane" dialog, which had in reality never been scripted into the movie.

Bob laughed, patted her cheek. The fantasy of the future ebbed away, and was replaced by the moment—this moment with her.

She frowned, then patted his cheek, smiling.

Then she touched her stomach, looked out at the cave entrance, and picked up her knife that was on the floor a little ways from them.

The implication was complete.

"Food!" Bob said. "Food!"

She frowned and then repeated the word. "Food!"

Standing and without a word or glance back at him, Tallie moved to the cave entrance, picked up her bow and the quiver, into which she put a handful of arrows that were on the floor beside it, then moved out of the cave.

Bob stood, startled, walked to the entrance, and looked down.

"Tallie!" he called.

She turned, smiled. "Food!"

Then she rushed down the pathway, and finally to the ground below. Bob watched as she disappeared into the jungle.

Sitting down, Bob wondered if she really connected the word "food" with hunger or with eating, or what. It was quite obvious that she made some kind of connection; that showed keen intelligence. Even then—was it possible that she had memory of a previous life before being in the jungle? That implied that she might have been a lost child—it all fed into his writer's imagination. What a story that would make! A bit of investigation might reveal her true identity.

If they could continue to survive in this jungle, together, maybe life wouldn't be all that bad. A primitive existence, of course; but better than death.

God, Bob realize, *I've changed!*

In his mind's eye he was now the creature his books had suggested him to be; the true adventure writer.

Am I mad? he wondered. *Maybe. Madly in love with a jungle goddess...impossible. But that's exactly how he felt!*

Survival was all that counted. And if they did....

He'd be with her. With his Tallie! She'd be his and his alone. Anywhere in the world; civilization or the jungle! He didn't care any more. It was madness, but such delicious madness.

He would teach her English; attempt to show her how to verbally communicate. She was quite obviously teachable. And, perhaps, she was some lost child and had memories to draw upon—deeply hidden in her subconscious mind.

He mused on that thought, wondering. Then other thoughts captured his attention.

What had happened to the rest of the group? Were the still alive?

The fantasy shattered.

Bob realized that somehow he had to find Rita, Carol and John Barton, if they lived. Depression settled down over him at the thought of the three other whites. Weaponless, going through the jungle, it seemed fantastic that they could survive.

They didn't have Tallie!

Yet, it was fantastic that he had survived at all. Who knew what might follow. Surely in all this madness some kind of order, intelligence, was directing things. One could almost believe in a Directing God! Perhaps such a Divine Creator did exist—and was on their side. Maybe God had a purpose for Bob Lake, after all! The thought was somewhat disquieting even while being something for which to desperately reach.

For but a moment Bob found himself whispering in the back of his mind a silent prayer for survival.

By the time Tallie returned to the cave with a couple of small tropical birds, Bob had made up his mind about two things: one was to teach Tallie as quickly as possible to speak, even if only a few key words and phrases; the other was to somehow attempt to find the others. There was a good chance that Tallie had the ability to track and might be able to pick up their trail.

But *first things first.*

He had to find some way to communicate his wishes to Tallie. Some way to let her know what he wanted.

CHAPTER 13

Rita's Last Stand

Rita awoke.

John Barton was sleeping. Carol was sitting up, watching the fire. The two of them had been taking turns sleeping and keeping watch. The moon was high. The cool breeze of the African night was chilly around Carol. They had dragged Rita close to the fire so that when she finally stirred and opened her eyes, Carol was able to watch the woman's features.

Carol's hands went instinctively to the spear that Barton had made for her. She was ready for an attack or a friendly greeting.

Rita sat up, startled, her face puzzled. Her features moved from questioning to a slow sagging expression.

"Carol," she said in a small voice. "I'm..."

"It's all right, Rita," Carol assured the woman, guessing at the meaning.

Rita sat there for a moment and then moved closer to the fire. "I don't—don't know what happened. I've always been a twit. Life hasn't been easy for me, no matter what you all think. Rich spoil lady. There's more to it, believe me!"

Her eyes met Carol's, evenly; there was a sharp spark of shame in them. "I admire you. Truly. A self-made woman who has succeeded in every way!"

Carol felt sorry for the other woman, regardless of what had happened a few hours before. What had pushed Rita over the edge was something neither of them might really know.

Her hand relaxed on the spear shaft.

Rita saw the move and suddenly burst out laughing. There was just an edge to it, a sharp cutting fine line that might have been humor or something else less easy to define.

Carol decided to laugh, too. Best to humor the woman.

"I'm just a crazy bitch in heat, I suppose!" the woman admitted. "Well, something like that. And a bit off balance, too! At least that's what all the head shrinks always told me! I'm humiliated...forgive me?"

All Carol could do was nod.

The two women laughed for a few moments.

John Barton had jerked up, wide-awake and cried: "What the hell's going on here?"

They turned, looked at him, suddenly quite serious.

"I'll never understand women—one moment they are at one another's throats and then acting like old school chums!" Barton cried, standing. "Better put some more wood on that fire—we don't want it to get down too low."

The women did as told and when the fire had burst hotter, Barton said: "You two sack out. I'll watch for a while."

As they lay down, Barton picked up the spear and stood over the fire, like a guardian giant.

His eyes moved from one woman to the other. They were so different. Rita, a rather voluptuous demanding, selfish, yet lushly passionate woman—but somewhat unnerved when faced with real hardships—or death. And Carol, on the other hand, was delicate, sensitive—intelligent; and amazingly strong, brave when the situation called for those qualities.

This was the kind of woman a man could easily fall for—John realized he was strongly attracted to her; but refused to give that any serious consideration. This was hardly the time to entertain romantic or sexual fantasies. Their survival depended on too much—and they had far too little to rely on. He needed to focus on nothing else but survival.

It had been a mistake leaving the plane crash site; rescue might have come. But the chances were too slim; without radio contact, how could the authorities possibly know where they had crashed. There was no doubt that when no word came from him, as was his habit when setting up camp, his office would notify the authorities that he was missing—possibly crashed. That might have taken days before they were found. It had seemed reasonable in the beginning to start out, attempt to find some kind of civilized outpost. But it wasn't! He shouldn't have listened to his companions' arguments. Now he wished he'd stayed. Bob would be alive; they would have some kind of protection in the night; arms, shelter.

* * * * * * *

Rita Bentley lay there captured in the last moments before consciousness returned.

It was an old dream of....

A strange form leaned over her, a hand reached out, touching her naked breasts. A murmur of pleasure shivered along her spine, into her groin as a soft voice said: "You're too lovely."

That voice shocked her to the core as another hand searched under the blanket. She recognized it.

"Too lovely for other men!" It was drunk, and slurred. "Just like your mother!"

Rita was slowly aware her surroundings, as consciousness ebbed back. The flood of anguished memory choked at her guts.

She wanted to escape all that; forget. Never dream again.

Oh, God...help me! The anguished plea came from deep inside her, reaching out to envelop every thought. She couldn't take it any more. If only she'd had some of the pills to dull the overwhelming mood shifts.

The old depression deepened, this time mixed with hopelessness. They'd be killed by some savage beast or by a band of natives. Or just starve. Maybe quick death was better.

She felt lost; tangled in a black, ebbing black monster of her mind. It was impossible to escape that horror.

She let her eyes glance at where John sat before the fire, the newly made spear in his strong hands.

The well of confusion folded down around Rita, once more, driving her deeper into the old horrid pit.

She felt feverish, light headed and strangely distant from her normal self. Her thinking was fogged.

Dark Rita was getting so strong!

Suddenly she knew there was the only one final answer. She had tried it before; failed. But this time, maybe it would work! There was nobody to stop her; and maybe the moment had come!

"John," Rita's voice called out to him in a low whisper.

The man watched her stand, outlined by the flickering light of the fire.

Her lips parted, as if to say something, but instead a low animal scream of anguished desperation came from them.

Carol was already on her feet, behind Barton and Rita's eyes found her.

The woman charged at them like a wild jungle tigress.

Barton quickly moved, the spear came up between him and Rita, threateningly. He didn't actually plan to use it. Things happened so fast then that it was impossible to stop them.

Rita moved directly toward its deadly, fire-hardened tip.

John Barton attempted to lift the point, move it away from the woman's path. He was a split second too late.

The sharpened shaft slid easily into Rita's soft belly. Blood spurted from the wound and she slumped, falling to the ground, a low agonized groan sounding from her mouth.

Carol covered her face. "Oh, my God!"

John recovered from his shock first. He quickly

knelt over the dying woman.

Rita looked up at him, her face drawn white, her features almost relaxed, as if the pain was not even bothering her.

"Why?" John choked out.

Rita's full lips trembled, her eyes seemed to plead for understanding, then fluttered and closed.

* * * * * * *

Bob managed to get a fire going from some twigs and matches he had. Tallie was frightened by the match at first and then fascinated. She insisted on taking one and striking it against the ground. When nothing happened, she frowned and looked at him.

Bob showed her how to strike and hold the match. When it lit into a flame as she struck it against the match pack, she laughed happily and danced around.

Bob pointed to the match and then fire, said: "Fire. Fire, Tallie. Fire."

She repeated the word then laughed again. Her eyes sparkled in the darkness like two little flames.

Later, after having cooked one of the birds, he showed Tallie the meat and managed to get across to her that she was to try it. She grabbed the cooked bird and jerked off a large piece of meat with her teeth. After a moment she laughed and took another bite.

Bob had managed to teach her a couple of words while they were fixing the meal, and was amazed how well she caught on.

After they had eaten, he set about attempting to get across the idea that he wanted to join his friends.

After endless motioning, drawing on the cave floor, Tallie smiled, her way of saying yes.

Then, in hand motions, she "spoke" to him. Her hands made a sun, as she said fire, acted out the sun falling over the horizon and then coming up. She smiled, then curled up on the ground next to him, almost immediately falling asleep.

For a long time Bob sat there, thinking, wondering if he was doing the best thing. Then a thought occurred to him. If she could return to the site of the camp, he'd be able to get his holster, which had been lying by his blanket that night he'd been captured by the natives.

His thoughts blurred for a while, and he was sure he had fallen asleep. A little later he watched Tallie sleeping next to him, curled up as close as she could get.

Tender, gentle thoughts played around his brain. He had never known a woman like this; he had never dreamed it possible to know such innocence. So different from other women. As he thought about Tallie, the mental picture of Carol Hill jarred the image away. Startled, he realized suddenly how much his attitude had changed about life, about women, about his future. Before, he had looked upon Carol as an attractive female he might make love to. As to Rita, well, she was like so many others, a body to enjoy; usually when he was half plastered, not feeling much more than erotic desires.

Bob realized he hadn't had a drink for many hours. Strangely enough, he didn't want one. At least at the moment. Maybe never again!

All he wanted was this woman with him right

147

now.

He caressed Tallie's forehead, gently, so as not to awaken her.

But her eyes opened, looked up into his, her lips smiled and then she fell back to sleep.

Sometime after that, Bob fell asleep and then, when he awakened it was light out, the sun just tipping over the edge of the world, the birds singing in the jungle forest surrounding the cliff side.

It was a beautiful sound, a beautiful world to which he awoke.

He lay there for some time, just listening, then must have fallen back to sleep for when he awakened again the sun was higher in the sky and Tallie was gone.

Bob stood, startled. Where could she have gone? What could have happened to her? Then he realized that she'd spent all her life in the jungle and surely knew her way around.

It was some time before she returned and the sun was high in the heavens.

She carried berries and nuts that gathered in the jungle. She placed them down beside him and then smiled, offered him one of the nuts after having cracked it open with her knife.

Bob was just reaching for it when a sound that wasn't of the jungle caught his attention.

Tallie heard it too, because she jerked up, looked out the cave opening, into the sky.

Neither of them moved for some time.

Bob didn't want to believe he was really hearing that sound. Civilization so close—yet so damned far away!

148

A plane. But it sounded strange, different.

Bob stood, moved to the cave entrance.

Tallie pointed off to the north, her face bright and happy.

A helicopter.

Bob's heart jumped. That could mean only one thing. Barton had been right! Rescue would come, in time. The plane would be found and then what?

If only he had his revolver. That would attract attention.

The helicopter was flying half a mile east of them, going south, too faraway to possibly even hear a gun shot. They were flying low, slowly as if carefully searching the jungle underneath them.

Then, suddenly the helicopter started circling. At first Bob believed it was turning about, giving up a search that had taken them so close to the wreckage, then he realized it had found the crashed plane. The copter lowered and then disappeared behind trees.

Bob pointed to where the copter had landed and then nodded to Tallie.

"Tallie," he pointed to himself and then to where he wanted her to take him. "Bob, there!" He pointed again and again until she smiled, grabbed hold of his hand, and started to pull him down the pathway.

He hesitated for a moment, looking at the cave where he had found something so beautiful, so fulfilling that he never wanted it to end.

He felt a sense of regret; then suddenly remembered that he could take Tallie with him back to civilization. There she could be taught English, and after that, tell her story. And the two of them would become famous as a result of the book he planned on writing.

149

What a story! Bob thought, excitedly. Then he realized that this wasn't his reason for wanting to take Tallie with him. His reasons went deeper, much deeper. He didn't want to lose this jungle girl, he didn't want her to go out of his life.

It didn't even occur to him that Tallie might have anything to say about that. They started down the path along the side of the cliff and then finally onto level ground and into the jungle.

CHAPTER 14

Final Rush to Rescue

Carol felt cold inside. It didn't seem possible that Rita Bentley could be dead. It had happened so fast, so unexpectedly. She could hear John Barton covering Rita's unmarked grave. Carol found it hard to keep the choked sensation of tears from her eyes and throat.

I'm being a baby!

The scraping of earth stopped and John Barton walked toward Carol.

"It's over," he said, simply.

Soon the two of them might end up dead, without any grave to protect their bodies from the savage jungle beasts.

Neither of them moved for a long, long time. Finally Carol said: "What could have caused her to do a thing like that?"

Barton shrugged. "Damned if I know. She did it on purpose—I mean, falling into the spear point— wanting to die!" His voice was full, lower than normal, a little shaky. "God-darn if I know why."

He was now standing so close to her. Carol hadn't even been aware of standing to meet him. Yet at that moment they were so close they could easily touch one another. The thought of being held close to him was overwhelming. She never knew exactly how it happened, but his arms were around her, and she was thrillingly hugging tightly to the man. His firm body was like steel fire, making her heady with sudden desire, almost drunk with it. How easy to just strip naked and let him ravish her. Rita was dead. They were alive. Life could be ripped away in one bold stroke. Morality be damned.

All that counted was this moment, this frantic desperate mutual need, beyond which nothing else mattered.

She saw the driving desire in his eyes as they looked down into hers, a powerful force eating over every nerve like some liquid fire.

It was happening too fast to even think.

He drew her closer, and she lifted her parted lips in hunger, wanting to feast on his. She felt the world slipping away, turning into a sea of sensations without any real shape or form, only the endless pleasure flushing over every nerve. His hands and lips seemed to flow over her flesh, lingering, tasting and thrillingly discovering a sense of her.

Carol was totally drown in the pleasure of his search along the sensitive nerves, the tender caressing that drove her further and further from the horrors to the wondrous joy of being completely possessed by this devouring male beast! Oh, she loved it! She loved him. She wanted to scream that into the world, but only moaned in delirious pleasure. She was swimming in that eternity of joyous ecstasy in his arms, without even knowing what their bodies were doing, other than being so close, so near, so flushed with mutual wanting, desire and fulfillment. She had never wanted anything more in her life! Just escape in his wonderful embrace.

Carol was aware of the moment of penetration and after that only of the continual wave upon wave of joy that raged through her again and again, driving her further and further down an endless whirlpool of sensations that were totally overwhelming beyond anything she had ever imagined. In the final moments it was a complete fusion of their bodies. The aftermath came slowly in lingering waves.

She didn't know how much time it took to refocus her mind from the wonderful pleasure of being held in this man's arms and the sense of security she'd known during those amazing moments.

The murmur of jungle birds fluttered through the air. It was the only sound for a long, long time other than their breathing.

Then another sound caught Carol's attention. At first she couldn't identify it. Then, it grew louder.

John Barton stood, looked up into the sky.

The sound came closer.

"A plane!" Carol shouted, her fingers gripping Barton's arm.

"No...more like a copter!" His voice was bright, excited sounding; there was hope in it for the first time in days.

They stood there for a moment longer and then John Barton turned, faced Carol.

"There's a chance," he told her in an even voice.

"A small chance. They might—they'll find the crashed plane, then possibly come down, investigate...we have to take the chance they'll wait...come!"

They dressed without so much as a comment as to what had happened between them. It was as if that prolonged shared mating was so natural that neither needed to explain or excuse those actions. What it might mean for the future was not the concern of the moment.

Without waiting for her to say or do anything, John took hold of her hand and headed in the direction the copter had been going. When the copter seemed to circle, the sound fading and swelling, fading and swelling, Barton stood, listened carefully and then changed their course into a more easterly direction, toward the circling copter. Then suddenly the sound faded and cut out.

"They've found the plane," he told Carol, holding back the branch of a bush so that she was able to go through the underbrush without being hit in the face.

They half ran, where possible, went at an agonizingly slow pace when the jungle was too thick to allow a faster pace.

Insects buzzed around their sweating faces and they swatted at the hungry creatures that kept coming back and back and back.

The minutes dragged into eternities. It was an endless world of jungle, insects, heat, underbrush and the desperate hope that they would somehow find the rescue party still at the plane crash site; an impossible hope to which two desperate humans were racing against time to make come true.

154

Barton was always in the lead, his hand held the spear—the one which had taken the life of Rita Bentley, ready for an emergency which might unexpectedly come.

The sun moved across the sky, baking down upon the torrid lands like a gigantic heater, burning the flesh, squeezing it dry. Sweat would break out over their flesh only to sizzle away.

Carol's mouth was dry, a large desert, her muscles almost exhausted to the point where it seemed impossible to make the next step. But she managed the impossible.

Only one more step, she would tell herself, just one more and then another.

She didn't think about the distance they were attempting to cover as fast as possible. She didn't worry about the dangers which might lie between them and their destination—or the amount of steps they had already taken. All she thought about was taking that next step. She attempted to ignore the insects and the heat and the exhaustion.

Then, suddenly, she stumbled, fell. She tried to move, but couldn't; attempted to get to her feet, but not a muscle would move.

"John!" she managed to moan in a weak voice.

The man stopped, turned, moved to her, then suddenly picked her up in his arms, and continued through the underbrush.

"You can't do this!" Carol told him.

"Quiet!"

"Leave me here."

"Shut up!"

The man staggered through the underbrush, always, instinctively managing to keep in the same direction.

For a long time he continued to carry her, continued to move toward their destination. And finally she found herself so aware of his naked flesh against her own. He was powerfully built; the muscles of his chest and arms thrilling hard, undulating against her. She could feel his heart beating. She was alive with so much longing and desire caused by all these sensations. Carol feasted on every moment, dreaming of being once again made passionate love to by this strong, desirable male animal. It was in this dreamlike state that she found herself floating, almost half asleep, as he continued to carry her through the jungle. Her own arms had slipped about his neck and she remembered what it had been like with him captured so deeply within her embrace. How she longed for him again!

Those thoughts drifted after a while as semiconsciousness rocked her almost to sleep.

The sun dipped low, close to the horizon before John Barton finally came to a stop, exhausted. What had kept him going that long Carol would never know.

They settled down by a tree trunk, Barton gathered small twigs, started a fire, put several pieces of wood in the flames and then fell exhausted onto the ground.

Carol watched the man. He fell asleep almost immediately. She caressed him with her eyes, taking in the strong, hard muscles on his back, shoulders and arms. It had been wonderful being held in those arms, feeling the hard muscles play against her.

She wasn't aware she had fallen asleep, but suddenly she was wide awake, and it was completely dark. How long she had slept, she didn't know. Groggily she laid there, her head braced against the tree, trying to think, trying to realize that there was hope, to convince herself they actually had a chance. But it seemed almost as if they were drowning people reaching out for a straw that couldn't possibly hold their weight. The copter and all the hope it brought would certainly lift away, unknowingly leaving them behind to face death. Or, maybe they'd make it there in time. If not, John Barton would be the last white man in her life. The two of them would be trapped in this jungle for the rest of their lives, together. That thought strangely enough wasn't as horrifying as she'd have imagined. Being with John was hardly undesirable. She moved closer to him. The awareness of very real longing and need soothed her, blanketed the more realistic fears. Her mind drifted, then she was aware of the man's body pressing closer to hers.

"John," was all she said, eyes not even opening, though her lips were half parted.

"You're so...beautiful!" he murmured, then suddenly he folded himself totally around her. There was no uncertain hesitation. John Barton simply took her as a lover might, confident in her total submission to his need.

Neither of them spoke words, but the sounds that uttered from deep within them became a melody of love.

For now, surely, they where true lovers.

When Carol fell asleep again, it was with a sense that the man really wanted her as much as she wanted him. That first time had not been a mere accident, a mere mutual sharing of momentary need. How long the need might last was impossible to tell. But for the moment they were committed to a relationship that might not have much of a future, but was mutually shared.

The next morning they again said nothing about their lovemaking, but did share a momentary embrace, a lover's kiss, before starting off through the jungle.

* * * * * * *

And while Carol Hill and John Barton were racing against time and against hope toward the plane crash, that afternoon Bob Lake and Tallie made their way through the jungle in a straight line toward the crash site. To Bob, each step seemed to take forever. To Tallie it was annoying to her to be forced into walking through the underbrush when she would make far better time in the trees.

The sun went across the heavens and then tumbled down to the horizon. Just as it started to get dark, Tallie squeezed Bob's fingers, smiled, and pointed through the underbrush.

There before them, some twenty feet away was a flickering fire.

Bob felt his heart jump into his mouth, and then like a man saved in the last moment from horrible death, he leaped forward, rushing through the underbrush, leaves slamming his face, small branches cutting his legs and chest and arms. But he felt nothing other than the insane joy of what he was seeing.

He broke into the clearing, fairly laughing with happiness, and then came to a stop in front of the fire, falling exhaustedly.

"Thank God!" he moaned to the two men sitting by the fire. "Thank God!"

They leaped to their feet. "Where are the others?" one asked.

Bob shook his head. "I don't know. Somewhere in that blasted jungle!"

For a moment they looked at one another and then the tall, gray haired man, said: "I'm Allen Gordon—Barton's partner—and this is Eddy Eisen." He pointed to the young, sandy haired man by his side. "We thought it better to stay the day and night... just on the off chance. What happened?"

Like a child, Bob started telling the story of their adventure. Then he remembered Tallie.

Stopping, Bob suddenly turned, searched the jungle around the clearing.

"Tallie! Tallie! Tallie!" he screamed, suddenly frightened that he would never see her again. And he knew at that moment he how much he needed Tallie; he wanted to be with her for the rest of his life.

Rational or not; that was his total conviction. Book be damned!

Hope crushed away. Then there was rustling in the tree above the clearing and Tallie swung down onto the ground, smiling. She came over to him and hugged close, as if frightened or bashful. Bob put an arm around her. He wanted to kiss her, to tell her how much she meant to him, to make love to her.

But there wasn't anything he could do other than smile and hold her.

After a moment he continued his story, telling about their capture by the natives and the escape. He ended with:

"If they're alive, they have to be out there some-where!" Allen Gordon nodded. His wrinkled face lined tight, thoughtful, his eyes became distant. "I'm surprised at John—he should have stayed here!"

"He wanted to...but we outvoted him."

Again Gordon nodded. "When we didn't hear from you...well we started searching. Believe me—that's a job. First you have to go over the same line of flight and—well, we were just lucky. We decided to stay this day and night, then tomorrow give it a go in the air, searching for any sign of you, hoping the engines would attract your attention."

"They attracted my attention this morning—that's why I'm here now. Maybe they'll..." Bob swayed, his voice faded and died, his vision was suddenly blurry. Exhaustion had suddenly set in,

"How about a snort?" Eddy Eisen offered, pulling a half empty bottle of whiskey from the camping bag.

Bob nodded, took the bottle, gulped. The liquor tasted strange; almost unwanted. At the same time a slow sense of well-being set in to his exhausted nerves. At least, for now, he'd needed that.

Then he sat down again, close to the fire. Tallie sat next to him, warming herself with the flames. If he could have her, he'd need to cut down on the boozing.

That thought was surprisingly embraced without any hesitation. Bob realized that a major change had altered his thinking about life.

The two other men hadn't been able to keep their eyes off Tallie for some time.

"A striking girl," Gordon announced, while openly admiring her nude young body so brazenly offered for all to see.

Bob felt a wave of jealousy shoot through him. Suddenly he wanted to cover Tallie's nakedness so that the other men couldn't see her. But that would be impossible and silly, he realized. Clothing or nakedness really didn't mean much here in the jungle; but it would when they got back to civilization.

For some time the two men questioned him about Tallie and then wondered between themselves the same things Bob had been wondering about. How could a girl like Tallie possibly have survived in the jungle? Where had she come from? It was a mystery that couldn't possibly be solved until she'd learned to speak—and maybe not even then.

One thing he determined to do was take her to civilization with him. The very idea of what the modern world would seem to such a primitive little savage, who hadn't ever seen anything other than the jungle, intrigued and fascinated him. Everything would be new to her. Was it possible for such a creature to survive in that world?

Never mind that, Bob, he told himself. *Things will work out, even if I have to bring her back here and—what?*

Could he leave her now forever lost to him?

The very thought was disgusting. Somehow things would work out, he told himself.

The drink had picked Bob's strength up a little, but after a while the exhaustion ebbed back into place and suddenly he felt his head spinning with disconnected thought. He slumped. The last thing he heard was Gordon's voice saying: "The poor devil, what he must have gone through."

JUNGLE GODDESS, BY CHARLES NUETZEL

CHAPTER 15

Safari's End

Bob awoke refreshed. The sun was baking down upon his body, warming through his nerves, soothing the still tender flesh where the natives had tortured him.

The first thing he was aware of was the smell of frying eggs and bacon. The aroma sharpened his sense of hunger. He opened his eyes.

Gordon and Eisen were sitting by the fire, waiting over the frying pan.

"Hungry?" Gordon inquired.

"Starved!" Bob sat up. Then sudden fear jarred him. Tallie wasn't anywhere in sight.

"Where's the girl?" Bob cried, standing.

"She went off...sometime ago—I don't know where," Gordon told him. "We tried to stop her, but it didn't do any good."

Bob thought that over for a moment and then realized that she had probably gone off to gather breakfast, as she had the day before. A thin smile broke his lips at the thought of Tallie uselessly looking for food, when there was no doubt plenty for all in Gordon's supply. So much for her to learn! And he'd teach her everything she needed to know!

"What are the plans for today?" Bob inquired a few moments later as Gordon handed him a metal plate with three fried eggs and four thick slices of bacon. It seemed like the grandest meal in the most expensive restaurant in New York to Bob.

"Think we might take the copter up for a while, and then...look around for some sign of the three. They can't be too far, considering what you told me," Gordon said. "One of us should stay here, just in case they show."

"I'll stay put. Tallie might not be back by the time you guys want to take off." Bob hesitated. "How much of a chance do you think we have?"

"To find them?" Gordon shrugged. "It's a thick jungle. We have to hope they'll find us—or find a way to let us know where they are. Barton should think of something...and—"

The twanging of an arrow, thudding into Gordon's plate of food, cut off his words.

The two leaped for their guns, as Bob flattened himself against the ground. The old fears teased him, then flooded away as his eyes searched for the threatening danger.

* * * * * * *

Tallie had been happily moving through the middle terrace of the jungle trees, freed of the confining underbrush that had slowed her progress the day before with Bob Lake. She was happier than she'd

164

ever been in all her life. Never before had she known such a wonderful thing could happen to her. If Tallie had known about love, and understood it, she would have understood the emotion she was experiencing. In a strange way they had bonded in their mating games—and she understood something about the need of one person for another of their kind.

A soft murmuring sounded from her lips. It was hardly a melody but as close as she could come to it. A wonderful sensation was bubbling in her heart and she was happy.

How long she had been moving through the trees, Tallie wasn't aware. But suddenly her sharp sense of hearing picked up a sound that wasn't native to the jungle. Immediately she froze, standing on a thick branch. She looked down at the jungle under-brush below her.

A man and woman pushed through the game trail.

Tallie watched them for a moment and then quickly scampered down the tree, and dropped onto the trail before them.

* * * * * * *

Carol Hill jumped, as if shot. For a moment she was too surprised to say anything, then sudden joy leaped through her; why she didn't really know. Maybe because this jungle girl had been a God send that night when she'd led Bob and herself back to camp.

The naked girl motioned to them, her lips smiled.

"Tallie... Tallie," she announced pointing to herself. Then she motioned them to follow her.

Barton gripped hold of Carol's hand. "What do you think?"

"It's better than...maybe she knows what she's doing," Carol suggested.

John Barton shrugged and they followed the jungle girl along the game trail.

Just then they heard the sound of gunfire, just a short distance from them.

Gordon's voice shouted: "To the copter—fast!"

* * * * * * *

Bob Lake came to his feet, rushed toward the copter that was sitting in the middle of the clearing. Just as he was about to reach it, a native leaped out in front of him. A spear menaced Bob.

Unlike the man he had been just days before, Bob leaped into the attack, sidestepped the spear thrust, then swung at the pointed black chin. The many fun times boxing in the gym focused his actions. At the same time he grabbed for the spear. Jerking the weapon from the other's fingers, he rammed the point into the man's chest.

Gunshots sounded, shouts pierced the jungle air.

Bob turned and saw Eisen go down with an arrow in his chest.

Gordon rushed toward him. "Into the copter!" the man shouted.

Bob made the dash, covering the three yards in two leaps, then pulled himself up into the copter. He searched for a weapon and found a rifle stacked

166

against the far wall. Grabbing the weapon, he turned, started firing at the half dozen natives rushing Gordon. The white hunter came into the copter, slammed the door shut bolted it.

"You know how to run one of these things?" Gordon asked.

Bob shook his head.

"I've watched Eisen." The man shrugged his broad shoulders. His old face lined. "Well, we're safe in here, in any case! I'll radio for help! It'll be some time in coming—but we'll get out of this damned mess, yet. If only Barton were here!"

The natives were hammering on the door with their spears and fists.

Gordon turned, aimed his rifle, and fired through the metal.

The hammering stopped.

Bob watched out through the door window as the natives backed away and then slowly melted into the jungle.

"They're gone!" Bob announced.

"The hell they are!" Gordon laughed. "They'll stay out there until doomsday! If only I could fly this damned thing!"

Bob was looking through the window at the camp, when suddenly the foliage opened and Tallie stepped into the clearing followed by two others.

His heart leaped, excitedly.

"Gordon—Carol—Barton!" He flung open the door, his rifle ready; his finger squeezed a couple of shots in the direction in which the natives had disappeared.

There was a shout of pain and then a shout of

rage. Then the race was on.

Tallie leaped into a tree, Carol and Barton shot forward, running at top speed for the copter.

Gordon helped the woman up into the copter. An arrow just missed her shoulder, bounding off the metal side of the copter. Barton took a running leap then rushed to the controls.

Bob fired until the gun was empty.

Gordon had already started firing at the natives, holding them back. The copter purred, then roared, the propeller blades cut into the air above them.

Then a score of natives rushed in from the surrounding foliage toward the plane. Arrows and spears flew through the air. Some arrows came from a tree, high above the clearing, cutting into the backs of the natives.

Bob was reloading as he realized that Tallie wasn't with them. He shouted. "Tallie! Tallie!"

Just then an arrow slammed into his chest and he felt himself crumble down against the floor of the copter. The world spun dizzily. Pain seared his brain. In that moment Bob was convinced he was dead. And somehow that wasn't as horrible as the loss of Tallie. Then blackness ebbed away all conscious sensations.

The copter slowly rose as the door shut against the charging natives. Slowly it ground its way above the screaming savages and then soared upwards above the trees.

In moments it was shooting northward toward civilization.

* * * * * * *

Bob had been in the hospital well over a month before he was well enough to receive visitors. During the latter days he had plenty of time to think about his future; a future that seemed radically different and fuller than it might have been before having crashed in Africa. Those events had changed his life forever. He was a different man, eager to face whatever dangers might offer themselves up to be brushed aside by direction action. But even this new Bob Lake was helpless to one dream; one desire; one determination. Everything hinged on his returning to the territory where Tallie lived and finding her. And bringing the jungle goddess back to the civilized world.

The first day that he could have visitors, Carol and John Barton came into his room with bright smiles on their faces.

"Well, when the hell are you going to get well?" Barton demanded, as they settled down into chairs at his bedside.

"They say after a couple of weeks I'll get out of here."

Bob looked at Carol. She was beautiful, radiant. Her eyes were bright and happy; happier than he had ever seen her before. Something had changed her, too. She was more relaxed, more content looking, less frantic and driving.

"You've changed, somehow," Carol observed.

"I have. Somewhat," he grinned. "But never mind that."

"Oh?

"Well, mind it…I'll have a favor to ask."

"Anything," John offered generously.

"And," Carol said, smiling: "We need your help,

too, about something, Bob."

"What?" he frowned, looking from at the two smiling faces.

"Well," Barton announced, "You're the logical choice for the best man, considering all that we've gone through!"

"Best man for what?" Bob snapped back.

"A marriage ceremony!" Carol laughed.

Then he knew. "I'll be damned! I never thought—never would have thought it would—"

"It happened," Carol said, "the other night. Big White Hunter Barton popped the question like a nervous shy boy. I thought he never would." She beamed at the large man sitting next to her. "I guess he had me from the beginning, but I didn't know it until...a lot happened to us all." She was silent for a moment, then asked. "I guess you'll be going back to the States—and you can tell Turner that I'm resigning. That should be a shock to him!"

Bob grinned, thinking about his editor-publisher. "Why don't you wire him yourself?"

"Maybe I will," she laughed.

Bob sobered after a moment and then asked Barton: "What would it take to hire a copter to return? I want to find Tallie!"

Barton frowned, his eyes narrowed. "Are you serious?"

He nodded.

"We barely got out of there with our teeth! You almost didn't make it," Barton explained. "Why?"

"Why not?" Bob inquired.

"Hell, nobody would believe me if I wrote a book about these adventures—without the evidence in the flesh!"

Carol's eyes brightened. "What a book that would make! *Bob Lake and the Jungle Goddess*!"

"The exact title I had in mind!"

"Can I go with you?" Carol wanted to know.

Barton said in a soft but forceful voice: "NO!"

After only a short hesitation, Carol shrugged. "Big Bwana say no! No it is! You'll have to get some one else to do the photos for you."

Bob grinned. "I'm going to bring her back. You can take all the photos you want—then!"

Carol yelped, happily. "*Bob Lake and the Jungle Goddess*, with photos by Carol Hill!"

"Carol Barton!" John suggested rather firmly.

"Oh, I almost forgot!" she laughed, taking his hand. "Of course. Assuming, Bob, you mean it!"

"A promise!" Bob assured her.

Barton grinned, as his eyes met Bob's. There was a knowing expression in his features. "I take it you found something special in the jungle, too."

"I guess so," Bob announced. "I guess maybe if I can get the chance, I'll have to ask you folks to be witnesses for marriage, too."

"She's a savage!" John pointed out.

"But a woman," Carol noted with a grin at Bob.

The writer nodded. "I know, doesn't make sense. I mean, we may never be able to communication in a normal fashion. Who knows? But I'll keep to my fantasy. And hope!"

Carol winked at him, saying: "I suppose it isn't any more fantastic than the many books you've already written."

"And hard reality, this time around," Bob announced, unafraid to admit the truth. "We connected out there. We'll connect again, somehow. Only time will tell."

Barton nodded: "Assuming you find her and she comes back with you and…"

"Write another bestseller!" Carol offered.

They laughed happily, talked about their plans to form an expedition back into the jungle to find the jungle girl, Tallie. After a little while the doctor came into the room and ordered the visitors out.

Just before they left, Bob said: "John—go ahead and make the arrangements. The moment I'm up and about!"

Barton nodded seriously before the door closed between them.

Bob Lake lay back as the doctor examined him. Now that the first steps had been taken, he felt better. It was only a matter of time before he would have his little jungle girl in his arms again. The idea of marriage was fantasy, perhaps, but a nice one; and if possible certainly a promising one. Of course a lot would depend on that charming, innocent, jungle girl, Tallie. He didn't have the least doubt that he would be able to find her, or that she wouldn't be safe when he did— after all, she'd been in the jungle all her life—a few more weeks more or less couldn't make that much difference.

Once the doctor had left him alone, Bob lay back, closed his eyes, and mentally relived his intimate moments of love with the jungle girl. It wasn't long before he fell contentedly asleep.

Three weeks later he was out of the hospital; and the day after that he left the Nairobi airport.

Destination:
Tallie!

* * * * * * *

It was over a year later that the book came out, as illustrated with the photos taken by Carol Barton. It contained the adventures of Bob Lake's story of his daring rescue of the jungle girl from deep, darkest Africa. (Soon to be a major motion picture.)
The cover featured a picture of….

"The Jungle Goddess"

ABOUT THE AUTHOR

Charles Nuetzel was born in San Francisco in 1934, and writes:

"As long as I can remember I wanted to be a writer. It was a dream I never thought would materialize. But with the help of Forrest J Ackerman, who became my agent, I managed to finally make it into print.

"I was lucky enough not only in selling my work to publishers but also ending up packaging books for some of them, and finally becoming a 'publisher' much like those who had bought my first novels. From there it as a simple leap to editing not only a sci-fi anthology, but a line of sci-fi books for Powell Sci-Fi back in the 1960s. Throughout these active professional years I had the chance to design some covers and do graphic cover layouts for pocket books & magazines."

Much of his work in covers and graphics are a result of having had a father who was a professional commercial artist, and who did a number of covers for sci-fi magazines in the 1950s and later for pocket books—even for some of Mr. Nuetzel's books.

In retirement he has become involved in swing dancing, a long time lover of Big Band jazz. But more interestingly world travels have taken him (and his wife Brigitte) across the world, to Hawaii, Caribbean, Mexico, Kenya, Egypt, Peru, having a lifelong interest in ancient civilizations. His website is full of thousands of pictures taken during these trips.